Disturbance
in One Place

Disturbance in One Place

A Novel

Binnie Kirshenbaum

Fromm International Publishing Corporation
New York

Published in 1994 by Fromm International Publishing Corporation,
560 Lexington Avenue, New York, NY 10022.

Manufactured in the United States of America

Designed by Gene Crofts

Printed on acid-free, recycled paper

First U.S. Edition 1994

Library of Congress Cataloging-in-Publication Data

Kirshenbaum, Binnie.
    A disturbance in one place : a novel / Binnie Kirshenbaum.
        p.   cm.
    ISBN 0-88064-157-6 (acid-free) : $19.95
    I. Title.
PS3561.I775D5   1994
813'.54—dc20   93-46671
                                                          CIP

to Maureen H., thank you

My brother used to ask the birds to forgive him; that sounds senseless but it is right; for all is like the ocean, all things flow and touch each other; a disturbance in one place is felt at the other end of the world...

Fyodor Dostoyevski
The Brothers Karamazov

Contents

The Way Frankie Sings   3

Brooklyn *T*s   6

An Angel's Kiss   9

Check a Box   13

Making Beds   16

Awakening   20

Forgiveness   25

An Address   30

A Brief Outline of My Accomplishments   34

First Love, Last Love   41

Breaking Fast   49

Jews Have No Business Being Enamored of
Germans   53

The Ins and Outs of Committing Adultery   59

Sons of Enormously Wealthy Men   62

Guilty as Sin   68

wo

The Only Son   75

Separate Bags   80

Keeping Track   85

Beginning with Jealous Greek Goddesses   90

Another Crime of Passion   94

An Eye for What Looks Good   98

Mary Magdalene and Company   101

Matinee   105

To Know the Extreme   108

That Little Exchange   112

Seven Tales of Famine   116

Going for Distance   122

Another Hunger   126

Eye of the Needle   129

hree

An Out-of-Body Experience   135

A Parable   138

Contents

Mirror, Mirror   140

Why Is a Good Question   143

Part of My Other Life   147

Haircut   151

Under the Aegean Sky   154

Recorded Messages   159

From Inside the Bone   163

Grandmother in Wolf's Clothing   167

The Confidence Game   172

Heart Failure   175

In Black and White   178

Early the Next Morning   181

Forfeit the Kiss   184

Everything Passes   187

One

The Way Frankie Sings

I want to run, take up running for sport, maybe run marathons. With this in mind, I buy an outfit: gym shorts, tights, lycra tank top. I also get a pair of Reeboks and one of those leather pouches to wear around my waist, to carry the essentials, like money and a lipstick.

Washington Square Park is where I choose to run. Not actually in, or through, the park but along its perimeter. I go there at dusk when the purple sky, ushering in the cool of the night, offers reprieve from the August heat.

He's leaning against the post of a stop sign at the park's northeast corner. He's dressed in black, but not like the swarms of young punks straining for decadent in ripped T-shirts, and shredded denim. His clothes are snazzy, sharp. Lightweight gabardine trousers, a double-breasted linen sports jacket, like an old-time hood, a thug, a shadow cast. A briefcase rests on the ground between his feet, and I assume it's filled with packets of crisp money, or heroin, or a pistol with a silencer—the tool of a paid assassin. As I near him, I watch him watching me.

3

His eyes follow me, and when I pass, I feel him checking out my behind.

On my second lap around the park, he is prepared. He's got a cigarette out, unlit, between his lips. His glance catches mine, and he gestures the striking of a match. As a rule, runners don't smoke. Two steps away from him, a pair of teenage boys are smoking reefer. He could've asked them for a light. But it happens, along with money, a lipstick, a pack of Players, I've got a book of matches.

He looks on while I unzip my leather pouch as if it were my dress I were unzipping, as if I were doing something sexy. I fork over the matchbook, and he looks at it, both sides.

I might as well take a cigarette break too, and he strikes a match for me, cupping his hand around the flame. We stand there smoking, sizing each other up, but we don't speak. His steady gaze from beneath heavy eyelids leaves me somewhat unsure of myself, off balance. But I keep my chin raised, tilted a degree upwards. I hold my eyes steady, firm like his, and I blow smoke rings because I don't want him suspecting I am a little bit afraid.

My cigarette is nearly done, and I drop it, snuff the ember with my sneaker, and wait. I wait for him to say something, and he lets me wait. Another minute of that, and I think *the hell with him*. I'm about to take off, resume running, when he says, "Your matches." He holds them out for me to take. "Thanks for the light. I appreciate it." His voice, his diction, the way he enunciates his syllables, punctuates his consonants is unmistakably Brooklyn, elegant. He speaks like Sinatra sings.

Running, I've concluded, is not the sport for me. As something to do, I didn't care for it. The outfit is unattractive, and the experience of running around and around the park, with no destination, was all too reminiscent of a dog chasing its own tail.

Nonetheless, I return to the park at dusk. Not to run, but to prowl. I go looking for that man, that hit man, to find him if I can.

That he should be exactly where I left him the night before, at the northeast corner of the park, is farfetched. Yet I am not at all surprised to find him there, leaning against the stop sign, hands behind his back. "Got a match?" I ask.

He brings his hands around, not to light my cigarette, but to produce a bouquet of flowers, the way a magician brings doves from a silk scarf or thin air. The flowers are red. "I never did anything like this before," he confesses.

The sun slips below the horizon. Night falls, and we walk. It seems as if the city were deserted, as if he and I were the only two people, alone together, out on the streets. Our footsteps echo.

We ask no questions.

"I've been waiting for you," he says. "My whole life I've been waiting for you."

I hold the red flowers by the stems, and a wind rises up around us, a warm wind, a summer wind.

Brooklyn *T*s

*I*t's like a string of firecrackers popping off the way they do on Chinese New Year: powPOWpowtityPOWpow, or the rat-a-tat-tat of machine-gun fire. I can almost smell gunpowder. These are the orgasms the hit man gives me, the Al Capone climax, the St. Valentine's Day Massacre. "Snappy the way you Italians do things," I say.

"Hey," the hit man takes offense. "I'm an American. I was born here," although given the circumstances, he can't be too offended.

American. He considers himself American the way an ostrich sticking its head down a hole in the ground considers itself hidden. He clings to this delusion: Brooklyn is a part of the American landscape, like Bay Ridge is Ohio farmland, Flatbush a town with a main street and general store, as if playing stickball in a vacant lot under the el were the same thing as Little League baseball.

I prop myself up on one elbow and study his face. His skin is olive, his lips full, bowed, and his nose—a nose that would be a disaster on a woman—is strong. He has a lot of chest hair.

6

"So," he gives me a playful slap on the haunch, "how about a cup of coffee? You want?"

"Cawf-fee," I repeat the way he says it, the way he bites on his consonants, emphasizes his *G*s, *D*s, *S*s, and especially his *T*s, adding *T*s even where there aren't any, squeezing *T*s into words where they are not written, the way he says *altso* for *also*. He gives words jazz, syncopation. Is it any wonder, then, he gives me orgasms with riffs?

He gets up from the bed to make the coffee, but before going to the kitchen he puts on his underwear. Oh, what underwear he has! Magenta briefs and one of those sleeveless T-shirts, ribbed. Underwear that's crude, vulgar, base, unbearably romantic.

"How about you?" he asks. "You want something to put on? A shirt to cover up?" He suggests that next time I come I bring a robe, a housecoat he says, here to hang in his closet.

"No," I tell him. "I'm either dressed or undressed. No fig leaves for me."

I like my body naked. When I put clothes on, it's with the idea of taking them off. I wear dresses held shut by a single snap. A slight tug, an absentminded pull, and any of my dresses will fall open, slide from my shoulders to the floor as breezy as autumn leaves falling from a tree. I am easy to get to.

With this in mind, I never wear shirts with many buttons, tight jeans, pantyhose, shoes that lace, boots, nor use a diaphragm as a method of birth control. I aim to avoid slapstick.

Earlier this evening, when the hit man was over me, kneeling between my legs, he said, "Hold on a second."

I did not want to hold on even if only for a second. Some things can't be delayed without going stale, losing fizzle. He twisted around to the night table, opened the drawer, and fished out a foil packet, a condom. With resignation and pain he sighed, "I guess I better put this on."

This is the truth about using condoms: No one does. At least those of us not part of a high-risk group. Oh, we pretend otherwise, feign social responsibility, claim we use them religiously, but, in fact, we're careless, stupid in our belief that nothing awful can happen.

"I don't know about you," he tore at the foil with his teeth, "but I haven't been with anyone for a while. And that was a pretty long-term thing." Such was the case he pled.

"Skip the condom."

"What?"

"No condom."

"Oh, am I glad you said that. I'm no good with this rubber business," he made it sound as if a condom were an utterly confounding newfangled device he couldn't cope with, the way some people can't cope with fax machines, automated tellers at the bank, or contact lenses.

We went at it then, as if it were before, before the world became such a complicated and dangerous place, when man and woman had no fear of communicable diseases, no self-consciousness, when there was no original sin. We fucked as if we were in Paradise.

I watch him make the espresso, standing at his stove, wearing his magenta briefs, curls of chest hair climbing from the neckline of his sleeveless T-shirt. It's impossible to imagine I will, ever again, get excited, aroused, by Brooks Brothers Pima cotton boxer shorts, Hanes crew neck undershirts.

"You wanT somethinG elTse with the CAWffee?" he asks. "A sweeT, maybe? Or a piece of fruiT?"

Oh, how he sings to me, a siren's song. And I, in a foreign land, am enchanted, seduced by the cadence.

An Angel's Kiss

*T*he hit man is cooking dinner for us. Gnocchi sautéed with broccoli rabe in olive oil, heavy on the garlic. Fish salad that I suspect has squid, eel, octopus in it. Eggplant, ratatouille, only he calls it something else, by another name. "And I got a bread from Zito," he shrugs as if this were nothing, no big deal.

We eat off a card table set up in his one-room apartment. The plates are good china, ivory-colored porcelain. Pink roses garland the outer edges. I compliment them. "Nice plates," I say.

"They were my mother's," he tells me, and he makes the sign of the cross.

Despite his claim about being an American, the hit man is so Italian he refers to his heritage as Sicilian. This leads me to think he is in way deep, like Hasids dividing their camp into the Lubavitchers and that other one. I mean, really, what's the difference?

Yesterday, the hit man and I went to a café where he is known. The proprietor came rushing out from behind the copper coffee machines to greet him. *"Professore, Professore,"* the proprietor effused. He and the hit man spoke together in words of earth tones, words I did not understand. After the proprietor returned to his place, the hit man said to me, "Lovely people. Him and his wife. Neapolitans. Ricotta. The Neapolitans are ricotta."

I cocked my head the way a bird does. I didn't follow him, so he explained, "Ricotta. Soft. Warm. Like shit."

If I look up from my plate of gnocchi, I'm eye to eye with the crucifix hammered to the wall over his narrow bed. On a shelf is one of those holy pictures, the sort featured on religious Christmas cards or pinned to car dashboards.

I am Jewish, married, and left-handed.

I put down my fork, and the hit man takes my hand, pulls it to his mouth. He kisses my fingertips as if they were part of the meal. "Hmmmm," he says, "I love lefties." Then he lets my hand go and adds, "But I'm not always so enlightened."

He is part of something so thick there's no escaping it. To come from Brooklyn is to come from solid ground, a place with roots, with ties that bind. Although he crossed the bridge, came over, a lot of years ago, Brooklyn remains in his speech and in the way he sees things.

I envy him that. My Jewishness, about which I sometimes make a great fuss, is ersatz. As fake as paste. My people were of the diaspora. They assimilated, blended, melted in the pot until we were no longer distinguishable. The food we ate was from the A&P: Oscar Mayer hot dogs, Shake 'N Bake, Tater Tots. Of kasha, of kugel, of herring, my mother said, "Yech! Smelly Jew food."

So, I grabbed it—Jewishness—for myself, made it mine the way Liz Taylor and Sammy Davis Jr. did, only I was spared the hoopla of conversion. All I had to do, like the hit man, was cross a bridge. Except I came from the opposite direction. It was here I picked up a smattering of Yiddish, ate noodle pudding at the B&H on Second Avenue, roamed Brighton Beach, Williamsburg, searching for my *shtetl*, my bit of Brooklyn.

But it's not genuine and not really mine, and if I were ever to cook dinner, borscht and latkes, for the hit man, it would be false, not easily swallowed.

He is not really a hit man. He is a professor. Of history. American History. He's written books on James Madison, Alexander Hamilton. I find it curious he didn't study his own people, become an expert on Vespucci, Verrazzano, keep handy a pocketful of anecdotes about Fiorello LaGuardia. I ask why he didn't write books defending Sacco and Vanzetti, and he says, "That's not my area," as if he were a gangster talking about a piece of Philadelphia run by another gangster. Instead, he's fascinated by Jefferson, Franklin, Adams, guys who wouldn't have given him, a WOP, the time of day.

Yet when he speaks of the Federalists, he makes them sound like boys from the neighborhood. And he looks like a hit man, moves as if he's sparring. It is easy to picture him breaking kneecaps for a living. His eyes are a mosaic of greens, blues, grays, and the way a ray of sunlight comes through a stained glass window—in a hard, straight line—something cold cuts through his eyes. His voice, too, can take on a chill, except when he talks about me. When he talks about me, he sounds Neapolitan.

So fast and too much, he loves me. I never expected that. My error was to peg him as a guarded man who would keep me guessing. Now, I wince as I see the adoration in his face. I prefer when the shadows cross over, when he looks hard-boiled, tough, mean, when he pins my arms back before kissing me. Still, his kisses are soft. So soft. Brushing lips with an angel. There ought not to be such a tenderness about him.

We finish dinner, and he clears the table. I remain seated while he makes coffee, espresso in demitasse cups. On a plate are pastries that look like seashells. I've seen these pastries many times but have never eaten one. "*Sfogliatelle,*" he names them. "From Rocco's. You know, next to the fish store."

I bite into one. It's bitter. That dried-fruit-peel crap. Swallowing fast, I wash away the taste with coffee.

"You don't like it," he notes. He doesn't miss a trick. "You didn't eat the calamari, either."

"I don't eat meat," I tell him, and he tells me, "Calamari is fish."

Around him, it's impossible to be alone. He notices everything I do, and he remembers everything I say. His people have their ways.

Again, he takes my left hand and pulls me up so we stand together. He is big. I'm small. "All day," he says, "I think about you. I can't stop thinking about you. And I get this tremendous heat in my church," he pats himself and grins.

"Your what?" I ask.

"My church. My church." Then something dawns on him, and apologetically he says, "You know. My temple."

I feel like the Madonna, that he is going to lift me onto the shelf, place me next to the holy picture, light a candle at my feet. And I would stay there, perfectly still, except for the teardrop rolling down my cheek, and he would think he's come upon a miracle.

Check a Box

*E*very now and then, it floors me to find I'm one half of a couple who—while David Brinkley pontificates on the television—peruses the Sunday *Times*, brunches on bagels, cream cheese or croissants, marmalade. My husband is doing the crossword puzzle.

I squirm, uncomfortable, as if I were in a confined space where I don't belong. Petulant, I commit civil disobedience. I shun *Arts & Leisure, The Book Review, Travel*, the sections I'm expected to read. Instead, I pull out inserts, glossy packets of advertisements, coupons for 25¢ off a box of Tide, 50¢ off a vat of Velveeta. Opposite the free trial offer for Sani-Flush is a survey questionnaire.

Should I trouble myself to complete this survey and mail it in, I will be rewarded with complimentary samples of laundry soap, window cleaner, furniture polish. Useless junk, but I get a pen handy anyway.

The thirty-six questions are all multiple choice. There is no essay to write. The directions read: Check The Appropriate Box.

Box. Aside from the conventional definition of box—packaging for a gift—I've used *box* as a slang word, an alternative for *snatch*. But when the hit man told me, "You have a perfect box," he traced, with his index finger, an imaginary—but vivid—line, cutting across my belly, down my left thigh, over, and up again, making a square. That's what he meant by box.

The first few question are a snap, a gift:

1) Age: 18–26, 27–35, 36–44, 45–60, Over 60

2) Sex: F, M

3) Yearly Income: Under $16,000, $16,000–$40,000, Over $40,000

4) Number of Dependent Children: Zero, 1–2, 3–4, 5 or More. I cross out the qualifier *dependent* and check *Zero*.

5) Preferred Cleanser For Mopping Floors: Pine-Sol, Lysol, Lestoil, Mr. Clean.

I skip that one and go on to #6. "Would you say," I ask my husband, "I do more than two loads of laundry a week?"

"You don't do any laundry," he notes.

"I mean," I clarify, "do you think what we send out amounts to more than two loads?"

"Eleven letters," my husband has his own puzzle to do, "for *Dilemma*. Third letter *R*."

"Gordian knot."

"It's time for your show," he passes me the remote control, and I tune in *Sunday School* hosted by Jimmy Swaggart. I used to watch Jimmy Swaggart for laughs, the way I'd watch *Hee Haw*. It cracked me up how he'd condemn most everyone to the fires of hell as if God were as shortsighted as he was. And all along, way before the story broke, I knew he was porking babes other than his pert wife. Lately, however, I'm finding him less funny, just as, I imagine, early on in his career Hitler was considered a kooky guy with a goofy mustache, and then one day he was something else.

18) Do I Most Often: Bake a Cake from Scratch, Bake a Cake from a Mix, Buy a Cake Ready-Made.

19) My Favorite Hobby Is: Needlecraft, Gardening, Aerobics, Watching Television.

23) I Attend Religious Services: More Than Once a Week, Once a Week, Occasionally, Not at All.

That's a very personal question—private, sacred—and the possibility of a connection between devotion and Lemon Pledge unnerves me.

23) I Attend Religious Services:

On the television, Jimmy Swaggart, pointer in hand, is tracing the route Jesus took to Calvary. I check the box that reads: Once a Week.

24) While on Vacation I Prefer To: Sightsee, Go to the Beach, Go to Amusement Parks.

I crumple the survey and toss the ball of glossy paper across the room. It lands by the radiator. I'm embarrassed for myself, as if I failed at something that matters. I feel like I have parts missing. Women everywhere can answer all those questions, no sweat. They were easy questions, but still I got answers wrong.

In a kind of resignation, an attempt to be more like the woman who could've breezed through that survey without a hitch, not stymied by *Hobbies*, but wouldn't squander her time on something so idiotic, I lean over my husband's shoulder. "There," I put my finger on 46 Down, six letters, begins with *M* for *Crosspatch*. "Misfit," I know.

My husband pens the letters in the appropriate boxes, in the boxes where they belong.

Making Beds

*I*t should come as no surprise to my husband, or anyone else who's ever met me, that I'm oblivious to household clutter, grime, disarray. Had my husband not pointed it out, I would not've noticed the dust particles banding together, manifesting a principle of static electricity. Just as rubbing a balloon along your sleeve will adhere it to a wall, dust clung to dust, making dustballs. Dustballs that grew, grew large, reproduced. Extended families of them squat under the bed, behind chairs, cozy alongside bookshelves and table legs. Also, my husband mentions there's a ring in the bathtub, corn flakes behind the stove, and unidentified sticky stuff on the living-room floor. Exasperated, he says, "Let's call a cleaning service. Get a professional in here to take care of this."

Oh, the voice of reason. Such a sensible suggestion. Pity I can't go along with it. I refuse to have a stranger fingering my dirt, wiping up my spills, organizing my disarray, becoming privy to, intimate with, my garbage. "I get it," I say. "You want to exploit an unfortunate illegal immigrant. Is that your plan? Pay the foreigner pigeon feed to do the shit work?"

"You've got it all wrong." My husband says we'd pay decent, honorable wages, but it wouldn't make a difference if we paid a CEO's salary. I offer a suggestion of my own: Let's move. Go to a new apartment. A clean place. Grow fresh dustballs from scratch.

When I moved into my first apartment on my own, a cubicle on Perry Street, my mother and that idiot I've got for a stepfather gave me a gift: service for eight. China, silverware, stemware, soup tureen, finger bowls.

This gift inspired me to throw a dinner party. I bought wine, potato chips, and ordered up Mexican food. I didn't have a table and had only one chair, so standing up we ate our enchiladas and refried beans off my new plates. When my guests left, I went to tackle the dirty dishes, to scrape crusted cheese from forks, to wash lipstick stains off wine glasses, to scour guacamole from the soup tureen. The prospect was bleak and overwhelming. I couldn't properly face it, and so into an industrial-strength Hefty bag went my dishes, salad plates, dessert plates, wine glasses, silverware, the soup tureen. I hauled the lot of it to the end of the block where a dumpster was parked.

The next day I went shopping and bought two plates, two glasses, two forks, two knives, and a pair of spoons. Two I could manage.

As winter approached, I discovered my Perry Street apartment was cold and dark. I wrote up a list of items I needed: blankets, a lamp with extra light bulbs, another chair, a Mr. Coffee machine. I gave this list to my mother and said, "If you were wondering what I might want for holiday gifts."

This is what my mother and stepfather gave me for holiday gifts: a mauve cashmere sweater—cowl-necked—and diamond earrings. A half of a carat on each ear to keep me warm.

My husband is unwilling to consider moving to a clean

apartment. "That's absurd," he says. "I don't understand why you won't call in someone. What's the problem?"

"I'll do it myself," I tell him.

I know better than to attempt cleaning the apartment in its entirety, to even picture all that needs doing in five rooms would send me to bed exhausted, depressed, done before beginning.

One room at a time. I start in the bedroom. With the bed. Stripping it, I pull away the spread, take off the sheets, dump pillows from their cases. I kick the pile of used linen to a corner, out of my path and line of vision, and I get fresh sheets from the closet. They are wrapped in brown paper and tied with string, a neat bundle back from the Vietnamese laundry.

The fitted sheet goes taut over the mattress, sharp. I stuff pillows into crisp cases, place them at the head of the bed. I marvel at the results. It hardly looks like a real bed, like a bed people sleep in. Rather, it could be cold stone, marble, carved authentically. Museum-goers, questioning the medium, unable to resist, would reach out to touch.

Shaking out the top sheet, I am reminded of how I'd heard that Hasidic Jews make love with a top sheet layered like icing between the man and the woman. A sheet with a hole cut out keeps them apart while they have sex. While walking through a Hasidic community, I'd looked for such sheets hanging to dry on clotheslines, all the holes centered as if a hungry moth chewed through them in succession.

Not long after that walk through Crown Heights, I had occasion to have sex with a boy I knew to be pious, devout, sincere, and on the verge of decision between rabbinical school or law school for his future.

In his bed we kissed, touched, removed our clothes, and the top sheet slipped between us. This was it! It was going to hap-

18

pen! I was going to experience sex via a mouse hole in the sheet. A dream come true!

I got myself thrilled for nothing. It, the sheet between us, was a mistake, a tangle unintended, which he rectified by yanking the sheet away, dropping it to the floor. We fucked the way I'd always fucked: flesh to flesh, pooch to pooch.

Smoothing out, running my hand along the top sheet of my freshly made bed, I pause at the spot where the hole would be, if there were such a hole, if I were to cut one out. I imagine sex between a sheet would be like living in an isolation bubble, or like a mime trapped behind the invisible window.

Awakening

*T*he hit man pauses until the waiter finishes puttering with our water glasses and goes away. Picking up where he left off, the hit man says, "I'm serious. Like right now. It's hard. Okay, not a full-fledged boner. A semi. But it's there." As if it were akin to Snow White roused from a coma by a kiss, the hit man claims I've awakened his cock.

To verify the veracity of this quasi-erection of his, I reach down under the white tablecloth to feel for myself.

"Hey, cut it out," he knocks my hand away. "You put one finger on it, and I got no choice but to fuck you here and now. You want that? On this table?"

"Maybe," I flirt with the idea, with him.

"I'm serious. It's true. Ever since I met you, I've got this awareness of my cock. Like now I know, all the time, always, that it's there."

"Where did you think it was?" I ask. "Where else could it have been?"

"I knew *where* it was," his voice grows louder the way music gets turned up as the party grows more lively. "It's not like I didn't know how to take a leak."

The two women at the next table hear him, and all four of us laugh. The women are still laughing, but the hit man cuts his short, moves his chair in closer to me, shuts the interlopers out. "It's not that I didn't always feel it before. I mean, I knew it was there. But now it's like banging up against my leg. Like I developed a new limb. Like when I go to the gym, I ought to hook it up to a pair of barbells."

It must be reassuring to have such solid evidence of arousal, something firm to hold on to.

I tell him how on television, on the news, I once saw a weight-lifting competition for frogs. Scaled-to-size weights were hooked to the frogs' front legs. Turned on their backs, the poor things pumped iron. This was meant to be the cute human-interest story of the day.

"Yeah, well, people are assholes." The hit man's not interested in anything but his cock. He's fascinated by its flurry of activity. "Yesterday, giving a lecture, it got hard. Really. There I was talking about Franklin's diplomatic efforts in France, and bingo! Major hard-on. I had to go to the bathroom and throw cold water on the son of a bitch. And you see how it is when we're in bed. It used to be once, maybe twice in a night. But with you, three, four times in a short afternoon. I swear to you, I haven't had sex like this, like it is with us, since I was a teenager. Except for maybe that one night in 1987."

Because the waiter is at our table with our dinners, I don't ask about that night in 1987, although I probably wouldn't have asked regardless. I get fettuccine with sun-dried tomatoes. The seafood marinara is for the hit man.

"*Mangia, mangia*," the waiter stands over us, urging us to eat, to approve. The hit man tastes his, savors it, and then kisses his fingertips. "Perfect," he says. "My compliments."

After swallowing a second mouthful, the hit man starts to say something. "Nah," he decides, his shoulders hunched, allied in the cover-up. "I can't tell you that."

"Tell me what?"

"You really want me to tell you?"

"I don't know until I hear it."

"Well, okay. I, uh, in my sleep, you know."

"No," I say. "I don't know. In your sleep what?"

"Yes, you know. In my sleep. I, uh, while I was asleep."

"You had a wet dream? Is that it?"

He glances to the next table. Relieved the women didn't hear me, he admits, "Yes. Isn't that strange?"

"No. At least I hope not. Considering I'm good for a couple a week, I assume it's normal."

"You? You do?" He is incredulous. "In your sleep?"

I can't determine if it's me, in particular, causing such a reaction. Or is it the phenomenon of women, in general, having dream-state orgasms? He has demonstrated certain ignorances in regards to the inner doings of women. Like he thought douching was something all women did the way we all pretty much brush our teeth.

I clue him in. "Women have wet dreams, too," I say.

"Don't you feel bad about that?" he asks. "About coming in your sleep? Doesn't it make you feel bad?"

"No. It feels good."

"I feel bad about it," he says. "I don't want to come unless I'm with you." He talks as if there were a limited supply, as if a wet dream were an orgasm wasted, as if he'd shortchanged me. This is why, he explains, he doesn't masturbate. To jerk off would be an offense, an affront to me if some of his sperm wound up in a tissue.

"So," I'm confident, cocky, "who starred in this wet dream of yours?"

He laughs, "My aunt," and claps his hands together, an exclamation point to the humor he finds in that. "My cousin Gina's mother. The old lady with Parkinson's. Do you believe it? I'm telling you, babe. I can't get over this. And at my age." The hit man speaks of himself as if he were much older than he is, as if there were more years than the dozen between us. "Honest, I feel like a kid again." This newfound sensation, this re-awakening is, for him, the fountain of youth, a geyser erupting in a steady spray of jizz, pulling him back from the brink. "Ever since that second time I saw you, it's different down there," he motions at his groin.

"The second time you saw me?" I query. "Not the first time?"

"The second time," he is positive.

"Come on," I fish for flattery upon flattery, "when you first saw me jogging around the park, tell me you weren't thinking about ripping those shorts off me?"

He swears he thought of no such thing. And to make matters worse, he adds, "I'm not sure I noticed your body at all at that time."

"Oh? And what were you looking at then? My mind?"

"All of you. Your presence. Your aura. The whole package. There was something about you, and it didn't have to do with tits and ass."

"But if you had to pick one part of me, isolate a piece of my body, the part that excites you most, which is it?"

He studies me slowly, lingers with love and lust and hunger. It's impossible to eat fettuccine under such scrutiny.

"Your hands," he decides. "Your hands drive me crazy."

My hands. I hold them out, to see for myself. They are my mother's hands, although she is not a lefty. When she was young, my mother modeled her hands. Her hands were featured in magazines, on billboards, advertising lotions, nail-care products, detergents that soften hands while you do the dishes. My mother and I could be taken for unrelated strangers, were it not for our hands.

Weekly, I go to a manicurist, a Russian émigré whose fingers are stubby. Her nails are ragged. She bites her cuticles, but she is attentive to my hands, massaging them with cream, shaping, buffing fingernails that get painted a variety of reds, roses, cherries, plums.

My hands. That was unexpected, and the ambush sets my hands aflutter. The hit man gasps as he takes hold of them, gently, as if they were songbirds, feathery, fragile, and easily crushed to death.

Forgiveness

*F*or years, I did, with deliberate forethought, tell the following lie: Half. I'm half Jewish. My father came from Methodist stock.

This lie was believable because my father was not around to deny being a Methodist, and also we celebrated Christmas. At Easter, I, religiously, got a new outfit, complete with patent leather Mary Janes, a straw hat with grosgrain ribbons sailing down the back. My mother baked a cake shaped like a bunny, a recipe from *Family Circle*, and when she remarried, it was to a Unitarian. Our house was a colonial furnished in oak. Denying ourselves glitz or glamour, our immersion into the melting pot was as complete as a baptism. To claim I was but half a Jew hardly seemed a lie. But it was a lie. A serious lie, although not as serious as the lie I later told: I am devout, a practicing Jewess, almost Orthodox. If Jews had nuns, I'd be one.

My lies were not confined to issues of faith. I lied about anything, told tall tales with aplomb as if they were self-evident.

Lying came naturally. For me, there was no such thing as fact, truth unalterable.

Having been invited to a pool party to celebrate my cousin's fifth birthday, my mother took me shopping for a new bathing suit. My debut bikini. White netting over neon pink top and bottom. I also got a pair of sunglasses, baby-blue plastic studded with pale pink seahorses.

My cousin lived way the hell out in Queens, and the Sunday traffic was congested. I was the last one to arrive at the pool party, where I knew no one except my cousin—a disgusting child who had filmy teeth. Sashaying across the yard, my little girl's rounded belly jutting out over my bikini bottom, sunglasses shielding my eyes, I spread my towel on the grass. I stretched out, declining to join in on the ruckus in the pool, which wasn't built-in but a three-foot high circle of corrugated tin. "No, thank you," I said. "I can't. I'm not allowed," I told those Queens kids. "It's in my contract."

"What contract?" a freckle-faced, chubby girl wanted to know.

"My contract with the studio," I said. "I'm a television star."

"Yeah? What show are you in?" That fat, ugly, freckled girl was a skeptic.

I whipped off my sunglasses. "*The Mod Squad.* I play Julie's illegitimate adopted daughter." Coolly, I stared down the non-believer amongst us until she held her nose and submerged underwater.

Eventually I gave up telling fibs, and I discovered the truth. The truth, the absolute truth, has the same effect as a lie. Either way, no one really buys it.

Take the man I swear I love. I do love him. The truth is: He is the love of my life. But when I confess that I love him, he chastises me for telling falsehoods. No matter how urgently I insist I love him madly, completely, he won't believe me. He hasn't the strength to believe me. Whatever allotment of strength he's got left, he uses to keep going, to go on. Often, I've asked him, "When are you going to quit suffering?"

Sometimes a lie catches up with you. Because of him, I am much like the Jewish nun I once purported to be. My marriage to him is not consummated. The adoration is manifested in spirit only.

Because I have a date with him—a meeting in a café where we can be together, yet nothing much can happen—I go all out to look my best. I take pains with eye shadow, lipstick, perfume. My clothes reveal hints of body parts—a skirt with a slit, a decolleté blouse. The message is explicit: See. See what you could have.

When I first fell in love with him, he was an older man. More than twice my age. Eight years later, having crossed sixty, he is on his way to becoming an old man. His hair is going gray. His silver-rimmed eyeglasses are bifocals. The clothes he wears are the color of dung. The skin on his neck is loosening, and his narrow shoulders sag. He is tired, but not in need of a rest. He picks up his tea cup with two hands. Those hands I crave to touch me all over are dotted with liver spots.

At his beckoning, the waitress comes to our table. He orders for me, "A cup of coffee, American, for the young lady." His accent is of no place. It's the accent of the nomad, the exile, someone who learned English as a second language, learned it perfectly, exactly, with not a trace of the old world or the new. He aims to assume the manner of a man stateless and without a past.

At this same café, perhaps at this very table, four years ago he'd said to me, "Married women are quite desirable. More so than single women, I think." He made this statement off the cuff, gave it no more emphasis than if talking of the weather, as if mentioning it looked like rain.

I was the one who presumed this was a vital message, one of great importance. I consider him to be a connoisseur of women.

That night I said to another man, a man I'd been dating, "Let's get married," which was how I wound up with a husband. A few weeks after my wedding, the love of my life and I again met in this café. "Well," I said, "I suppose this is it, then."

He claimed not to understand. "What are you talking about?" he asked.

"I'm married now," I reminded him. "Therefore, I'm more desirable to you. That does come with implication."

"I said that? About married women? I don't recall having said such a thing. Well, even if I did, I must've meant excluding you. You have always been eminently desirable. It takes all of my strength to resist you."

I forgave him that. I've forgiven him all of it. I have even forgiven him his cowardice.

Not only have I forgiven, but I feign forgetfulness, too. As if it's never come up before, as if I were telling him for the first time, I say, "I love you best. Let's go off together. Come on, what's to stop us? Together we can vanish. We can board a plane destined for a remote island, live in a mud hut, eat mangoes, bathe in the sea, fuck each other blind. We'd be so happy."

His slight smile is capable of bringing a misanthrope to tears. "It's a game to you of some kind, this talk."

What I would like to say to him is: You've ruined my life.

But I'd never say such a thing because it would make him sad. Never do I want to be the cause of anything but pleasure for him.

Instead, I say this: "Picture yourself old. I mean really old. Older than you are now by ten, twenty years. Picture yourself feeble. Sitting there in your wheelchair, a plaid blanket spread across your useless lap. You'll regret what we did not do. You'll wish we had. But it'll be way too late. I don't want that to happen. I don't want you to have regrets."

"How decent of you," he says. "But it's way too late for that."

With ten minutes to spare before the clock strikes six, the love of my life signals for the check. As usual, he gives me two hours with him, what will be two hours on the nose. We came together at four, and at six he'll stand up, bend to kiss me, once, on the mouth. The love of my life is as precise as a Swiss watch.

I reach for the check, to treat him to something, anything, a cup of tea. Yet even this small token, this miniature gesture of affection, is denied me. "This is mine," he insists. "Next time," he adds. "You can treat next time." This promise, the promise that there will be a next time, is a promise I grab hold of as if it were solid, with sides, dimension. It is what I cling to, keeping me afloat while I drift. And all the more, I wish I could give him something other than my forgiveness.

An Address

While traveling on the other side of the ocean, or walking through ethnic enclaves in my own city, or flipping the pages of *National Geographic* in the dentist's office, I keep an eye peeled for people who look like me.

I look for my people, try to find where I came from, to locate the shared gene pool. Somehow, that detail—from which port my ancestors set sail—got lost, misplaced, hidden, swept under the wall-to-wall carpet. "We're Americans," my mother said.

"Oh, like the Iroquois, the Chickasaw, the Kickapoo, Americans."

"Don't be fresh," my mother warned. "We're American Jews." She made it sound as if we'd sprung, fully formed, out of the foam at Far Rockaway. My mother's take on our heritage isn't all that different from the way the love of my life implies he rose up, a young man, from a sidewalk on Central Park West.

"Before we were American Jews," I wanted to know. "Where did we come from in the first place?"

My mother guessed, took a stab in the dark. "We might be

Russian," she said, "because we're tall." My mother was picturing the cossacks. The cossacks were the tall ones.

"I'm not tall," I pointed out. Shorter than average, I'm a hodgepodge, a platypus of regional features: hair of an Asian, skin of a Dane, Mediterranean mouth. Once I saw my eyes on a Gypsy in Granada. I could be the result of Jews having been booted from one place only to be kicked out of the next. Or I could say my people, my kind, began in the Tigris-Euphrates valley and leave it at that. I could, but I can't. I want to know if my grandparents' grandparents lived in Minsk, Marrakesh, Milan. I want to spin a globe, place my finger on one spot, come to rest, and say, "There. There was home. My permanent address."

My father—my real father, not that yahoo my mother married on her second go-round—spent the last ten or fifteen years of his life living nowhere but hotel rooms. He traveled a circuit from Las Vegas to Reno to Chicago to Atlantic City, which was, eventually, his last stop. Owing more money than he could ever pay to people who don't abide by bankruptcy laws, my father went from the eighth floor—head first—out one of those hotel windows before hitting the pavement. His death was ruled a suicide, but I wouldn't bet on that.

Before my father took off to make a life playing against the odds, he was a doctor. A hematologist. He knew blood. You wouldn't expect a hematologist to, one morning, kiss his wife and child good-bye, go to his office, clean out his desk, and vanish, only to surface from time to time at OTB parlors, at back-room poker games, and—when flush—at the baccarat tables.

But that's what he did, and although I barely remember him, I am my father's daughter. It's as if I too live in hotel rooms, a night here, another night there, always looking over my shoulder. And although I haven't hit, I do float, hovering somewhere between the eighth floor and the pavement below.

31

I expect the hit man—so firmly rooted in the soil of his people that the soil might as well be quicksand—to have sympathy for my plight. I'm practically an orphan. A person with amnesia. Oh, I remember all sorts of things—how to walk, talk, think, add and subtract, read, write, fuck—but there's this blank area, a place I can't recall. I grope to know it, but it escapes me.

"Hey," the hit man says, "we're Americans. That's it." He makes the same red-white-and-blue noises my mother does.

"No. We're not just Americans. You're not. First, we're something else. And I don't know what. I don't have a homeland. I don't have a permanent address."

"So what?" It's easy to dismiss what you've got. "What does it matter?" He knows not only that he is of Italian descent, but Sicilian. He knows the village in Sicily where his grandfather was born. And when he went to that village, he walked the same streets his grandfather walked, and knocked on the door of his ancestral hovel. "Tell me why this disturbs you," he asks.

I don't talk about the floating, the groping for something not there. Instead I say, "I don't get a parade. The Irish have St. Patrick's Day. The Puerto Ricans have their parade. Your people got dibs on the Columbus Day festivities. What do I do? Wear a button that reads: Kiss me. I don't know what the fuck I am!"

The hit man laughs, "You're mine. How's that? That's what you are. Mine. And you live in my heart."

His heart is not a permanent address. However, I let the subject drop. Perhaps I'm making too much of it. Perhaps the longing will pass.

The next day the hit man and I meet up in the park, at the base of the statue of Garibaldi. The hit man opens his briefcase, takes out a piece of paper, yellow legal pad paper, and gives it to me. I read: Box 3547, GPO, New York, NY 10087.

"What's this?" I ask.

"Your address," he says. "Your permanent address." The hit man has rented me a post office box. "So no matter where you go, you've got a way to touch base. Isn't that what you wanted?"

A Brief Outline of
My Accomplishments

waft from one painting to the next, gliding through clusters of tourists and art students here for the Rauschenberg retrospective. I stand before a huge canvas, but I'm looking at a man making his way over to me.

Something about this man is familiar to me, as if he bears a strong resemblance to someone I know, someone I am fond of.

"What do you think?" he asks, and I know he means about the painting. I shrug.

He tells me his name. In certain circles, he is somewhat famous. He's an artist. A multimedia artist, and I have heard of him, although I'm not familiar with his work. Judging from the way he stands—artificially bashful with a sheepish grin in the wings—I suspect he assumes I'm going to gush, as if I were a fan, as if he were really famous.

The silence is awkward, and I expect him to move away from me, but instead, as if we were at a cocktail party, he asks me questions: Do I live in the city? Which part? Where did I go to school? Did I do graduate work? With whom did I study? Where am I from originally? What do I do with myself exactly?

All his questions could be answered simply by giving him my résumé.

When he runs dry of things to ask, I offer, "Perhaps you'd like to check my teeth?"

He walks off, and I imagine that is the end of that. Only, somehow, we hook up again, downstairs, at the Calder mobile.

In his loft, I sit on a chair, nipping at cheap brandy from a Saucy Shrimp glass. He drinks apple juice from a jelly jar. He doesn't drink alcohol, he tells me. Or coffee. He doesn't do any drugs. He doesn't smoke cigarettes. "I don't have any vices," he says in a way that makes me defensive. "And," he adds, "I've been tested. I'm HIV negative."

A brush stroke of decadence, a small indulgence, perhaps impulsively buying some decent drinking glasses for a lark, just to be wild, might be the ticket to move his bowels for him. He is a rigid man.

"When I first decided to be an artist," he explains himself, "I observed that losers fell into three categories. Those who drank. Those who did drugs. And those who relied on spontaneity."

"You talk a lot," I note. I didn't come to his loft to feign interest in his theories on art and artists. "What do you say we cut to the chase?" I stand up and step out of my dress.

If there is one thing I excel at, it is giving head. I give good head. No, I give great head. I'm a professional when it comes to performing oral sex. This ability is, in part, a gift from God. A talent I was born with. I started out as a thumbsucker, but not any ordinary thumbsucker. My thumb was savored, slurped, trimmed, twirled, blown. I also delighted in putting objects in my mouth—coins, toy parts, balloons, door knobs—feeling, knowing, the shapes, textures, with my tongue.

Despite natural proclivities, giving great head is something I've worked at, practiced at every opportunity, honed to an art form. There are fine points to master: tongue rolling, flicking, when to be gentle, imperceptible, and when to apply pressure, and—the cutting edge—how to swallow with grace. I swallow beautifully, which, I've gathered, makes me something of a find.

The hit man told me, "Oh, not the way you do it, babe. No one's ever done it that good." Then he said, "In Brooklyn, we used to say, there are two kinds of girls. Those who do it for you, and those who do it for themselves. Later," he added, "when I went out with Protestants I learned there are some who won't do it at all."

Protestants is what the hit man calls anyone with thin blood.

"And which kind of girl am I?" I asked him.

"One of a kind. I'm telling you, babe. No one's ever made oral love to me like you do." That's what the hit man calls a blow-job—oral love—which, to me, sounds both romantic and obscene at once.

It matters to me that I give great head. I care. I want the men in my mouth to pant, "Oh my God. I never...Oh God, thank you...this is the best."

Giving great head compensates for giving a lousy hand-job. Because I'm left-handed, I'm not manually dexterous. Although left-handed women are no longer thought to be witches, we are a minority discriminated against. Desks, scissors, and fountain pens aren't designed for us. I was taught to throw a ball with my right hand, where there isn't any natural strength. All sorts of things were thrust into my right hand where they didn't belong: forks, pencils, tennis rackets, bowling balls, cocks.

When I was younger and knew next to nothing, a boy loosened my fingers and said, "Let me show you how to do this."

Oh, the mortification! The humiliation! How could I have been doing it wrong?

He took my right hand, guided it to jerk him off properly, but my hand went gimpy. This was not the trick for me. I let his cock go and nose-dived between his legs. I took him in my mouth and went to town. Instantly, he forgot all about the crummy hand-job. But I didn't forget.

Eager to show off what I can do, I run my tongue, a lizard's flick, from the multimedia artist's neck to his knees. Tacking back to his belly, I come in closer, closer, toying like a cat with a mouse, pawing softly before the kill.

He clears his throat, and I listen for the whimper, for the groan, for the pleading, the begging. "Um," he says, "that doesn't do anything for me."

I lift my head. I must've heard wrong, but he repeats himself. "Not you personally. Just that. It never does anything for me."

And I think: What is he? Some kind of queer?

I'm hardly about to go where I'm not appreciated, but what do I do now? Out of my element, I ransack my memory to locate another act, but if he's squeamish about having his cock sucked, he'll never go for the alternatives. At a loss, I roll over, pull him on top of me.

While he basks in the afterglow, I ask him a question or two. I don't ask the first question that comes to mind: What is your problem? But I do ask, "Do you consider yourself a more or less traditional kind of person?"

He looks around his loft, panning the space the way a video camera would, pausing at the canvases—splotches of spilled acrylics—stacked against the wall. His bookshelves are crammed with dense journals: *Diacritics, Neoliterate, Deutsche Zeitschrift für Philosophie, Context and Experiment.* These are journals I've occasionally picked up, thumbed through, and wondered, "Does anyone actually read this tripe?" Coming from his quadraphonic speakers are sounds of keening, chanting over atonal notes periodically climaxed by the crash, the crunch of automobile accidents. I am surrounded by examples of profundity that escape me.

"Obviously," he gets haughty, "I'm hardly status quo."

So I tell him I'm married. His face crumples. He's more status quo than he figured. "What are you?" he asks, "A bored housewife? Am I the equivalent of a bridge game or an afternoon at Saks?"

"I have no idea," I confess. "Maybe, but I wouldn't swear to it." Then by way of apology for my deceit I say, "I suppose I should've told you first," meaning before we went to bed, maybe while we were still sitting on chairs, or hanging out by the Calder mobile.

"Yes," he says, "you should've told me sooner." He makes my omission sound like another vice.

"Would it have made any difference?" I am curious.

"I can't answer that. It's hypothetical." And right then he gets hard again, pulls me over for another whirl. Let him act as high, holy, pure as he chooses. Between my legs, I'm keeping score.

Afterwards, I light a cigarette. There's no ashtray in sight. Nor does he offer to get me one, so I make do with the leftover inch of brandy in the Saucy Shrimp glass, and I say, "There's more."

"More?"

"Someone else besides my husband. Besides you." I tell him about the hit man. Not about the hit man in specifics. Just that there is someone else, someone else I have sex with. I don't, can't, lump the love of my life in with any others.

"So I'm number three," the multimedia artist is peeved at the billing.

What I'd like to say to him is: No, no, you're number eleven. Or seventeen. Or one hundred and sixty-two. But I don't. "That's it," I say. "You're number three."

He looks miserable but also titillated. Because, I've a hunch, he's a competitive fellow, he says, "You do realize I've been around, too."

"I should hope so." I drop what's left of my cigarette into the Saucy Shrimp glass. The ember hisses as it hits the brandy. Bits of tobacco float like fish food.

"Yes," he says. "I've been around quite a bit. And I've been involved with married women before. The thing I don't like about married women is how manipulative they are."

This tells me something: He's lying. He has never been with a married woman before. Not ever.

I lean over the side of the bed, place my Saucy Shrimp glass on the floor, and sit up. "I'm not manipulative," I say.

"I'm sorry. You're right." He apologizes for the stereotype but not for the lie. Anxious to change the subject, he looks at his watch and says, "I have to be at a party soon. Would you like to come with me?"

"Thank you, but no. I can't."

While we dress, he asks me what my husband does for a living, what degrees does he hold, is he famous in his field?

It would be fun to say: Perhaps I'll bring him by, and you can check his teeth.

But I answer his questions and observe as he tabulates credentials. The way beads on an abacus click, slide, slide, click, click, slide, tally, he weighs his accomplishments against those of my husband.

As if I could see, make out, the words collecting on the tip of his tongue, he's desperate to ask about the hit man, but I shoot him a look that warns: Don't bother. I won't talk.

Heeding my signal, he asks something else. "Can I see you again?"

I turn to him, and in the process, I kick over the Saucy Shrimp glass. It doesn't break, but cigarette remains—tobacco, ash, soggy filter muddied in brandy—spill out. A small, but dirty, puddle. "Sure," I say, and forging ahead blindly I step into the mess I've made.

First Love, Last Love

I wake to the rain—heavy rain. A glorious day for sleeping. Intent on spinning myself a cocoon, I pull the covers over my head when the telephone rings. It's the Kessel sisters calling, although only one of them, the youngest, is on the line. "Come over," she says. "We're having a party."

The Kessel sisters are a unit. I refer to them as *Kessel to the Third Power*. They used to be *Kessel Squared* before the eldest divorced the actor who starred in a series of deodorant commercials and moved, from Los Angeles, in with her two sisters, completing the triangle.

As close in age as possible without being biological freaks, each Kessel sister looks remarkably like the other two. Tall, thin, angular, with necks as long as wildflowers. Their blond hair falls in waves, ripples down their backs. From behind, it's impossible to tell them apart, except through smell. The eldest refuses to use deodorant. When they turn around, face front, they are all eyes and cheekbones. They resemble Modiglianis. Startling to look at and very beautiful.

41

"A party?" I ask. "It's morning. Isn't it still morning?"

"Yes," the youngest sister concedes. "We're having a girl party."

Girl parties are what we had when we were eleven, twelve years old, prior to blossoming into puberty. Such parties ended when boys, at last, became a reality in the flesh. However, girl parties were revived, occasionally, in college dormitories. Wearing our slobbiest clothes, gone-to-seed nymphs, we lounged around eating pizza, M&Ms, Pepperidge Farm cookies in repulsive quantities, drinking fortified wine from waxed Dixie cups. We talked about boys and sex, but danced with each other.

I stop at a liquor store to purchase my contribution to this party. A gallon jug of purple wine nestled in a basket. $4.99 plus tax.

Once before, a very long time ago, I bought this same wine as a gift for a boy I liked. I thought the basket made it special, a fancy wine. It hurts to remember such things.

I get off the elevator, and from 6E, the Kessel sisters' apartment, Leslie Gore is belting out, "It's my party and I'll cry if I want to, cry if I want to."

In delight, in unison, the Kessel sisters squeal at my arrival. I set the wine down on the kitchen table next to a Sara Lee coffee cake box, empty save for a few broken walnuts.

"Started without me, did you?" I say.

"Nah, we were just warming up." The middle sister is at the refrigerator, taking a tub of ice cream from the freezer. Chocolate Fudge Marshmallow.

The youngest sister rummages through the silverware drawer for spoons, while the eldest pours the purple wine into coffee mugs. There is no need—indeed, it would be counterproductive to our intent—to bother with niceties such as bowls or napkins or wine glasses.

We dig into the ice cream as if it were a fondue, a communal pot, and we snicker furtively because ice cream and wine for breakfast is disgraceful, shameful, and such good fun.

Another thing about wine and ice cream for breakfast is how we get tipsy in no time flat. The leftover ice cream melts in the tub as we sprawl out on the floor, on the couch, draped over a chair like last night's clothing.

"Let's make prank phone calls," the youngest comes up with a suggestion worthy of consideration until she adds, "like *Is your refrigerator running?*"

"Not funny," the middle one shakes her head.

The youngest, the most sensitive of the three, is pained by the rejection of her idea, so I aim to soothe her. "You're on to something," I say. "On the right track with the phone calls."

"Obscene phone calls." The middle sister wants to dial numbers at random, pant, breathe heavy, grunt into ears unknown.

Helping herself to more wine, the eldest sister makes an announcement. "In 1983 I had sex with a different man every night of the year. Three hundred and sixty-five days. Three hundred and sixty-five men. You can't imagine how slim the pickings were on Christmas Eve."

"Lucky for you it wasn't a leap year," the youngest sister giggles. "Imagine the sort of man you'd find on February 29th?"

The middle sister bounces up. "I've got it. We get some guy on the phone and say *I thought you ought to know I've got the clap.* Or those bugs that live in pubic hair. What do you call those? Scabies? Mange?"

"Crabs," the eldest knows.

"How about," the youngest is back in form, *"I'm pregnant and it's yours?"*

We laugh with abandon, spill over ourselves, hold our sides. We laugh this way not because such phone calls are clever, but because we once made such calls, and we recall the joy of them.

Eventually, the laughter dies to a hiccup, and the eldest Kessel sister hits on an altogether different plan: to unearth our first love. Remember him and then call him on the telephone.

"And say what?" the middle sister asks the same question I was going to ask.

"Say what we never said, what we always wanted to say but didn't."

Having shared years together prior to meeting me, the Kessel sisters reminisce, talk of boys before me, beyond me. I'm outside while they poke fun at the middle sister, at her first love, an eleven-year-old boy who wore Beatle boots and smoked cigarettes behind the playground slide at recess. "He was so cool," the middle one remembers. "A total moron. I was mad about him."

The eldest sister gets choked up recollecting a sandy-haired kid with freckles the size of dimes. "What was his name? Why can't I remember his name?" She implores her sisters to somehow bring him back for her.

"He wore plaid shirts, flannel ones," the youngest recalls a detail, "year round, even in summer."

"And he was frequently seen picking his nose," the middle sister rounds out the picture.

As if the Kessel sisters had a secret way of communicating, together, at once, the three of them turn to me. "You're awfully quiet," the middle one accuses. "Aren't you going to tell us about your first love?"

First love isn't definite the way a first kiss, a first fuck, a first husband is clearly fixed in stone. Without any formalities to pin love down, the concept can be fuzzy, so I pick one at random. I tell them the story of the teenage boy who drove a blue Mustang.

He, the teenage boy with the nice car, isn't where the story begins. To tell it right, I start with my discovery of the penis, first revealed to me by my cousin, the filmy-toothed kid from Queens. His mother, having herself a fling, needed to stash the kid someplace for the weekend. We got stuck. He bunked with us on a cot set up in my room.

Tucking us into our respective beds, my mother shut the door on her way out. My mother was asking for trouble.

The instant we were alone, my cousin asked, "You got any Magic Markers?"

Was he for real? Did I have Magic Markers? Name your color, pal. "Red. Blue. Light blue. Pink. Purple. Yellow…" I wasn't done listing them when he broke in, "Just a black one." My cousin had no pizzazz.

He followed me to my desk, breathing on my neck while I got the black Magic Marker from the pack. Grabbing it from me, my cousin hopped into my bed.

He clutched the marker with one hand, and with the other hand he pulled his pajama bottom to his knees. Hunched over, he kept his arm crooked, so I couldn't see a thing until he was ready to show me.

Upright, between his thumb and index finger, he held it. He'd drawn eyes on it, gave it a wide grin. The pinpoint hole sufficed as a nose. "Hi there," it danced, talked in a funny voice. "I'm Mr. Wiz. Ask Mr. Wiz a question. Mr. Wiz has all the answers. Mr. Wiz is a genius."

I was unable to ask Mr. Wiz a question. Mr. Wiz rendered me mute. I was overwhelmed by its existence, distraught, fascinated, furious. How did my filmy-toothed cousin land a puppet show in his pajama bottom?

Mr. Wiz sang, "Happy Days Are Here Again," which proved to be all the excitement my cousin could handle. When the song ended, he dropped off to sleep. I, conversely, was wide awake. Jealousy, profound jealousy, raged as an amphetamine.

I moved in closer. I picked it up. I flipped it to one side. And over. I tightened my grip. I poked, prodded, pulled, grabbed it by the throat.

"Owww," my cousin whined in his sleep.

I tugged, twisted, tried to unscrew it, but I couldn't find a way to snatch that doohickey to hide it in my dresser drawer under my socks.

All boys had one, this bone of contention. I coveted a penis more than I coveted any toy, including Creepy Crawlers and a three-speed Schwinn. Trifles compared to a penis. With a penis, I could go places.

Under the misconception that perhaps I did have one, one that was shy and needed coaxing to come out, I took to stroking myself. I won't say nothing came of touching myself, but it didn't win me a penis. In the end, I had to face the facts: I did not have a penis, and there was no way to get one.

I settled for escorting boys into the shrubbery and making them an offer: I'll show you mine if you show me yours.

If I couldn't have my very own penis, I did, at least, get the better half of that bargain. I got to touch the penises, pet them, wiggle them, waggle them, pinch their heads, kiss their noses. Whereas when I lowered my underpants, all the boys could do was look and note, "There's nothing there."

Abruptly—just like that—my obsession changed direction. Four- and five-year-old dicks lost their allure. I discovered big game, the teenage boy who lived across the street. He was dreamy. He drove a blue Mustang and had a summer job as a lifeguard at the country club. To this day, the combined smell of sweat, chlorine, and Coppertone generates a response in me, the way you can get a dog to salivate by ringing a bell.

Just before dinnertime, I parked myself on the curb, waiting for him to drive home in his car.

"How's my girl?" He picked me up, his muscles bulging. He tossed me in the air as if I were a football. Over his head, I spun, dizzy, and he caught me. "Oh," he said, "in ten years you're going to be something else."

In ten years, he'd be twenty-eight. I'd be fifteen, almost. That was too long to wait. The need to express myself, express myself then, swelled, throbbed, rose up with the urgency of desire. I could no longer contain it. I punched him on the arm. My baby-soft knuckles made contact with his rock-solid biceps. "Oh," he said, "you want to fight, do you? Okay, then. Let's go. Put up your dukes." He wanted me to hit him again. "This time, give me all you've got."

I did as I was told, and he went down, crumpled into a heap. He curled up, yelping. This caused a commotion on the block. Kids gathered around, and so did some of their parents.

"You broke his nuts," one boy accused.

It was an accident. I simply swung out. That I hit the bull's-eye was happenstance. I didn't even know about nuts.

A neighborhood father helped the lifeguard stand up, and my mother took me inside, sat me on the couch, and explained to me about testicles. "Men are very, very sensitive there," my mother said. "You mustn't ever hit a boy in that spot again. You could ruin him for life."

What did that mean? Ruin him for life?

"You could destroy his future happiness with women," my mother said.

Now, that was something to consider. "Do girls have a spot like that?" I asked.

"No," my mother told me. "Not like that."

✦ ✦ ✦

The youngest Kessel sister picks at the broken walnuts in the Sara Lee box, chews absently, stares off into space.

The eldest sister shakes her head. "I'm overcome with grief," she says. "That is the saddest story. The sweet innocence of your first love, and you turned it into something horrid." She takes hold of the jug of wine, pours some into her mug, half of which sloshes onto her hands and onto the floor.

"It was not my intent to make it ugly," I say. "It just happened."

"Doesn't it always," the eldest sister is near tears. "It's so sad."

"Sad?" the middle sister speaks up. "Sad? It was funny. How do you get sad from that? He wasn't even her first love, really." Often, the middle sister is perceptive.

"I have to throw up." The eldest sister carries her mug of wine into the bathroom.

Another cloud bursts. The rain runs down the window panes, clinging to the glass before falling away. And the youngest Kessel sister says, "Let's order a pizza."

Breaking Fast

*F*rom sunup, I am haunted by a sensation, a slight tug on the sleeve, like I've got a string tied around my finger whispering, *Don't forget*. It annoys me while I drink coffee, write an overdue letter, take a shower, get dressed.

I telephone the hit man. "Am I supposed to remember something?" I ask.

"Yeah," he says. "We have a date."

"No, no, that's not it. Something else. Am I supposed to bring cigarettes, or food, or wine?"

"I got everything," he tells me. "All I need now is you."

Aiming to jam more than sixty minutes into each hour, right away, before anything else, we fuck. Fuck with desperation, with urgency, as if we haven't been together for a long while, as if we fear we'll never be together again. We fuck as if one of us were going off to war.

Done, spent, the hit man is partial to hugging, snuggling close. He folds me to his heart, but I don't share his enthusiasm

49

for affection. On the pretense of needing a cigarette, I escape, slink from his grasp, and fish through my pocketbook.

I return to him, but I keep to the edge of the bed. I do not want to press my face against his sweaty chest. Catching my drift, he keeps his hands to himself and offers to make lunch.

He stands, puts on his underwear—turquoise briefs, black sleeveless T-shirt—and goes to the refrigerator. "How about a nice plate of pasta?" he asks. "I got some linguini here. A little butter. A sprinkle of Romano. Nothing fancy."

I'm not hungry enough for such a meal. "Something light," I say. "Nibble food."

He carries a tray to the bed. On a plate sit a bunch of grapes, two apples, and a knife. He feeds grapes, one at a time, into my open mouth, and slices of apple, too. When the fruit has been eaten, when all that remains is the skeletal stem of the grapes and the apple cores browning, he asks, "Coffee?"

With the coffee, he brings four slices of anisette toast. I take one, dunk it in the cup, let the toast soak up coffee the way a sponge would. This pleases the hit man, that I eat the anisette toast the way he does.

I can, and sometimes do, derive pleasure from making him happy. He is so easy to please. I put down my cup and saucer, take his from his hands and place it beside my own. Easing him back on the bed, under the sorrowful gaze of the sacrificial Jesus on his wall, I tug away his underwear and kiss his knees, thighs, belly, groin. He moans, and my mouth, open, wet, and eager, swoops over him.

How gratifying to have my praises sung! Cries of ecstasy! He pleads for me to stop, to go, more, oh please, and his eyes roll back in his head. "I can't hold it, babe," he says, and his gob jets into my mouth. I swallow, and it shimmies down my esophagus the way an oyster would. Like the oyster, it, too, is an acquired taste.

50

Allowing him to stroke my hair, I look up, past him to the window where I watch the sunlight shift and move in the direction of late afternoon. "I have to be going," I pull away.

It isn't modesty prompting the hit man to avert his eyes while I dress. He looks elsewhere, at the ceiling, the floor, the walls, because he can't bear to watch me prepare to leave him.

I don't, in fact, have to leave this minute. I could stay here with him until early evening, but I choose to go now.

The autumn air brings back to me the smell of burning leaves, of pumpkin patches, of harvests. Lovely memories from a childhood that was not mine. Still, such air invites me to walk, to linger, to take winding routes and side streets.

I stop at a stone building fenced in with iron railing. A synagogue. I can walk, have walked, these same streets day after day and yet, still happen upon something — a gargoyle, a stained-glass window, a courtyard, a trellis of roses, a synagogue — I've never seen before. Each step abounds with discovery, if, and when, I look.

I've never been on the inside of any synagogue, except on two separate occasions, when invited to Bar Mitzvahs to witness little boyfriends becoming men. And then I spent the better part of both services hanging out in the bathroom experimenting with eye shadow, cigarettes, and giving myself hickeys on the fleshy part of my arm.

It would satisfy a growing curiosity to step foot in this synagogue, to nose around and see what's there. I open the iron gate, but as if the ground before me has split apart and created a chasm, I can't get past the bulletin board. Black, cased in glass, white plastic letters affixed read:

Yom Kippur Service
Kol Nidrei

51

Mourners' Kaddish

Evening Service, Ne'illah

Yom Kippur. The high holy day. The day of atonement. The day to spend in meditation, prayer. The day of the fast. The day Jews are forbidden, by the law of God, to eat, drink, toil, play. The one day to compensate, to make up for all the others, and I, from the moment I woke, blew it.

I remain behind the iron gate, and my belly is full—full of coffee, grapes, apple, anisette toast, and a big gob of Catholic sperm.

Moments before the sun sets, shrouded in the velvet shawl of dusk, I hear the congregation's voices soaring in song: *Adon Olam Asher Malach Beterram Kol Yatzir Nivrach*. . . .

I'm not familiar with these lyrics, what they mean exactly. Yet the voices singing lift me off, far away. The song ends, and then the silence breaks, pierced by the blowing of the Shofar, the ram's horn. And I hurry into the night the way a watchful spirit vanishes.

Jews Have No Business Being
Enamored of Germans

*T*he multimedia artist has clogs on his feet, a fashion blunder I thought even the Swedes had gotten over. He also wears paint-splattered blue jeans and an insignia sweatshirt. I squint to make out the gothic lettering: *Universität Heidelberg.*

"Heidelberg?" I raise one eyebrow.

"Yes," he says. "I got this the last time I was there. Do you like it?"

"No," I tell him. "I don't like it."

He visits Germany regularly, often going to Berlin. Berlin is where it's happening, a forefront of a place, the artist's Mecca. He has many German friends.

"It doesn't bother you? Make you uneasy?" I scout for an ashtray. You'd think he'd have put one out, knowing I was coming over.

"It's a new generation," he excuses them, the Germans. "Besides, my friends are all artists and academics, scholars." He makes it sound as if only butchers and saloon keepers were responsible.

53

His affection for Germans confirms some suspicions I have about the multimedia artist: 1) he has a short and convenient view of history, and 2) he is cheap, tight with a dollar. Only cheap people can put up with the Germans, tolerate their stingy ways. The only things Germans do with largesse is plop potatoes on a plate and gas people.

The multimedia artist is taken with Aryan intellectualism. He's impressed by Heidegger, by Wittgenstein, by Kant. Logic, reason, ideas of the mind that get you nowhere.

"Did you know," I ask, "Kant was a virgin? His whole life and he never got laid?"

"Of course I know that. Everyone knows that. But what of it? The man was brilliant."

"He couldn't have been too brilliant," I remark. "Couldn't even figure out how to get some pussy."

"He hád a higher calling," the multimedia artist defends his idol.

Jews really shouldn't have Germans for idols. Not that the multimedia artist is all that Jewish, although a German wouldn't have made such a distinction. That the multimedia artist was Jewish at all did come as a surprise to me. That he and I have exchanged intimacies, bodily fluids, is a case of mistaken identity on both our parts.

When I first met him, he looked familiar. He does look familiar. He looks like me. Of him I could say: We are of the same place. His features, too, are from no one land but from everywhere. He shares my coloring, although he wears his black hair in a ponytail. When I'd asked him, "Where are you from?" he said, "Minnesota." There are places in the world I never imagine having Jewish populations: China, Honduras, Bali, Minnesota. I thought American Jews were pretty much confined to New York, California, with a smattering of us—having conked out halfway across the country—in Chicago.

54

I hadn't a clue the multimedia artist was Jewish until he brought the subject up, asking me, "What's your ethnic background?"

"Jewish," I said.

"You're kidding?" He was even more distressed than when he'd learned I was married. "I never get involved with Jewish women."

"Why?" I asked. "What are you?"

"Jewish," he said.

"From Minnesota?" My mind was reeling from the anachronism. "Were you the only one?"

"No," he said. "There were a lot of us. Not that being Jewish meant anything. We were all very assimilated," he said, as if the Jews of Minnesota had come over on the Mayflower, had Jews been allowed aboard the Mayflower. Then, as if I were supposed to say thank you, he said, "Well, you don't look at all Jewish."

"You're a new experience for me, too," I assured him. As a rule, I steer clear of Jewish men. As a rule, perhaps, but the love of my life is a Jew, although that's a feature of his I have to remind myself of because he, too, has forsaken it. "Your husband's not Jewish?" the multimedia artist asked.

"Anglo-Saxon," I said.

"And the other one?"

With all its implications, I intoned, "Sicilian."

It is the foreigners, the others, the outsiders, who find me exotic, rare, a wonder to behold. Such men do not point to my painted fingernails and cry, "JAP!" Only Jews have such contempt for their own, the kind of contempt that results in becoming enamored of Germans.

Jews have no business being enamored of Germans. We ought not to tangle with them. I know this from history and from experience.

I was fifteen years old, staying in a Youth Hostel in Amsterdam because I was on a Teen Tour and had no choice of accommodations. On this Teen Tour, I buddied around with a robust blond girl from Maine. We were a good team. Two pretty girls, but of such different styles, different tastes, that neither stepped on the other's toes.

Our last night in Amsterdam I had every intention of going to sleep early, but the blond girl from Maine came to me and said, "There's a handsome man in the Common Room. I want to meet him." The Common Room was what passed for a lobby in a Youth Hostel. She begged me to accompany her, to bolster her confidence. "Then you can go to bed," she promised.

He had shoulder-length hair. His fingernails needed cutting. He was twenty-nine years old, a biochemist, and was staying at a Youth Hostel instead of a nice hotel because he was a chintzy German.

When I woke up briefly at two in the morning, the blond girl's bed was empty. Good for her, I thought, although it was beyond me what she saw in some old hippie who wore clogs on his feet.

At breakfast, our packs leaning against our chairs for imminent departure, the blond girl from Maine said, "There he is. Come with me to say good-bye."

He wrote down her address in a worn leather book. "Und you?" He asked for my address too. Europeans, particularly Northern and Central Europeans, stress address exchanges. Spend ten minutes on a train with one, chat for two seconds in a café, and they'll whip out the address book. I used to think this was their way of being friendly. Later I learned it's because, should they wind up in your part of the world, they've got a place to freeload.

When my Teen Tour ended, I arrived home to find four let-

ters waiting for me. Letters from someone with a goofy name—
Fritz, Ralph, Kraut, Krupp—a name you might give a dog. He
wrote of his travels and how the Scottish Highlands—dark,
mysterious, haunting—reminded him of me, and I wondered,
"Who the fuck is this guy?"

Perhaps the blond girl from Maine could solve the riddle, so I
called her. "Yes," she knew. "The one I was with in Amsterdam."

"He must've mixed us up," I said. "Write to him and set him
straight, would you?" I had no desire to receive another skeevy
letter.

The fifth skeevy letter explained: No, he hadn't mixed us up.
My friend, the blond Christian girl, was very nice, but he wanted the Jewess.

I tore his letter into a lot of pieces before throwing it in the
trash. A month went by, when he called me on the telephone. He
was at Kennedy Airport, en route to California for a conference,
and wanted to spend the weekend in New York, at my house.

"I don't live in New York City," I said. "I live in a suburb. It's
not at all like the city. You can't see anything from where I live."

"I wish only to see you," he told me.

"Hang on. I have to ask my mother."

My mother's response was a shock, a cold betrayal. "Of
course he can stay here." She said we'd be happy to welcome
him as our guest.

My mother and stepfather thought he was a fine young man.
They liked his Ph.D., his manners. So polite. He complimented
my mother on her cooking, which only a German could do—
rave over meatloaf seasoned with onion soup mix.

"And what do your parents do for a living?" my stepfather
asked the fine young German man.

"My mother," he said, "is a librarian. My father is deceased. He
was executed by the Russians for war crimes before I was born."

57

I choked on a Tater Tot.

He excused himself from the dinner table to go to the toilet. That's how he phrased it—the toilet—which was disgusting, and I apologized to my mother for bringing Nazi offspring to the house. "I had no idea," I said.

"Don't blame the son for the father's sins," my stepfather admonished me.

"Oh, none of that concerned us," my mother waved off the Holocaust and a world war.

Very shortly after my mother and her husband went to sleep, the son of the Nazi came after me, sneaking into my bedroom. Although he didn't have a bayonet, he did have an erection that he pressed against me.

I pushed him off. "Beat it," I said.

"Excuse me?" His English wasn't all that great. The idiom wasn't in his vocabulary. To make myself understood, I had to shove him, hard, from my bed.

He landed on the floor, and rose up, but only to his knees. Kneeling, he reached out to touch me. "I am zorry," he whispered. "Please. Accept forgiveness. I am zo zorry."

Pity I was too young to appreciate the potential, the possibilities such an affair held open. A dominatrix daydream, and I didn't take advantage. Instead I said, "Get the fuck out of my room, creep."

He walked to the door and, before leaving, said lovingly, "Jew bitch."

Now, in front of me, the multimedia artist folds, neatly, his *Universität Heidelberg* sweatshirt and places it on a chair. I am fully clothed, and I step back to study him, his nakedness, his obliviousness to the situation: a naked Jewish man enamored of Germans.

The Ins and Outs of
Committing Adultery

*Y*ou're home early," my husband says from behind
the newspaper. For all he knows, I could be a cat burglar or a
succubus coming through the door instead of a window.

"It's almost seven," I take off my coat. "Have you had dinner?"

"A sandwich."

"Did you save me some Jarlsburg?"

"There's plenty left." He turns a page. The paper rustles.

I'm slicing a tomato when the phone rings. I cradle the receiver between my ear and my hunched shoulder. My hands are free to spread mayonnaise on bread, to unwrap the Jarlsburg from the cheesecloth while I find out what the multimedia artist could possibly want, given that I left him not twenty minutes ago.

He's called because he forgot to ask me if I'm free tomorrow night.

I hang up the phone and carry my sandwich to the living room.

"No plate?" My husband watches crumbs from the French bread fall like a light snow.

"That was the multimedia artist," I offer information.

"Who?"

"The multimedia artist. My friend who paints, sculpts, writes, composes, all in one ball."

My husband continues to look blank, so I say, "The one I spent this afternoon with. He called to invite me to an opening tomorrow night. Uptown. One of the 57th Street galleries."

"That sounds nice," my husband says.

The best method, the cleanest, safest way to commit adultery is this: Whenever possible, within reason, tell the truth.

The truth is liberating, not apt to do you in. The truth within bounds, that is. Do not be a well-intended fool. Do not say to your husband, "I'm going to be with my lover, one of my lovers. We're going to spend the evening fucking our heads loose."

But an even bigger mistake is to lie. I would never invent a sick aunt, never claim a Kessel sister is in distress and needs me by her side. Nor would I say I've signed up for an Italian language class that meets on Wednesday nights, for surely the day would come when my husband would say: *Allora, cara mia, parli un po d'Italiano por me.*

Lies, outright lies, have a way of looping to make a noose around your neck, or twisting and tangling over and under your ankles like a Chinese jump rope tripping you up.

Before you marry, it's best to be square with yourself on this question: Am I a runaround?

If the answer is yes, or even possibly, you'd be smart to get a husband who allows for extramarital entertainment. I don't mean a husband who'd go for one of those open marriages where you, your date, and your spouse all breakfast together the morning after. That's sick. Rather, pick a husband who likes that you have your own friends, your own interests.

Find a husband who is absorbed with his career, with a sport, or with a mistress.

Adultery is next to impossible if your husband is like a pet ferret, snooping, sniffing, curious. Also, it won't work if your husband is possessive and insecure.

Find a husband with a cold streak.

Keep your adultery clean, your stories streamlined.

It will be with impunity that I will meet the multimedia artist tomorrow night. I will stand around, drink wine, and listen to pretentious commentary without having to look over my shoulder. As big as this city is, circles can run small, overlap. But if it happens that I see someone I know, someone who knows my husband, at the gallery opening, there will be no cause for panic. No need to dash for the door or to hide out in the bathroom. I have not been duplicitous.

Carefree, I will return home, and my husband will ask, "How was it?"

And I'll say, "They served that lovely cheese. The kind layered with volcanic ash."

"Mobier." My husband knows his cheeses.

"Yes," I'll say. And then I'll confess, "I didn't like the paintings. Afterwards, we went back to the multimedia artist's loft, and he explained why they are important works of art, but frankly, I still don't get it."

"Well, it sounds like you had a good time." My husband will want to get back to whatever he was doing.

I'll screw up my face and say, "It was okay. Nothing special." That, too, will be so close to the truth, it will be honest.

Sons of
Enormously Wealthy Men

*H*e's got on an ugly jacket and a hideous tie. That his clothes are shabby, by 57th Street standards, doesn't register with him. Busy chomping on smoked salmon and crackers, he's bowled over by the goodies on the buffet table. "Imagine eating like this every night." The multimedia artist pops a strawberry into his mouth.

Strawberries out of season. I could've had such things. I could be running with the same crowd as George Bush, William F. Buckley. I shudder to think of it, and I try to recall: Did I ever boff a Republican?

Not to my knowledge. If I had, however, married that Skull and Bones boy, no doubt I'd have fucked scads of Republicans by now.

I'm including the Skull and Bones boy when I say I never fucked a Republican, even though I dated him for nearly a year. That's a mind-boggling fact. Naturally, I didn't date him—a boy who took six weeks to work up to a dry, shriveled kiss—exclusively. You'd get more tongue action kissing a puppy than you would from him. Only once did he touch my breasts, and so tentative a touch, I might've been mistaken. He was odd.

Weekends, I took the train to New Haven where he squired me to dinners, dances, tailgating parties before football games. At night, I slept alone in his roommate's bed. His roommate weekended in Poughkeepsie.

The crowd this Skull and Bones boy ran with was in dress rehearsal for middle age. The women they dated were thin-lipped, flat-chested, and without waistlines. In time, they'd have bodies like refrigerators. It was my belief no one in this crowd ever had great sex.

One Wednesday evening this boy called me up, his voice doing somersaults. He'd been tapped for a secret society. *The* secret society. Skull and Bones. He wasn't supposed to tell anyone, "But I had to tell you," he said. "This is the biggest thing that'll ever happen to me. I had to share it with you."

I'd taken up reading *The Nation, Mother Jones, The Daily Worker,* hawked by a very sexy blue-eyed Marxist on College Walk. Therefore, Skull and Bones didn't send tingles down my spine. Idiotic fraternal organization, not even egalitarian enough to go Greek.

"You must vow to me you won't tell anyone I was tapped."

"Who would I tell?" I'd be embarrassed to tell anyone I was dating such a boy.

I continued to date him largely out of curiosity. Was he ever going to attempt penetration? When, where, how would he make his move?

Each time, and there were dozens of them, he walked me by the Skull and Bones headquarters, he'd stop and say, "Well, there it is. That's it."

It looked like a mausoleum. Windowless, closed as a crypt, as if all those unfortunates not tapped for membership would've given their lives for a peek inside.

63

Having ducked out, at my insistence, of an absurd banquet, we were once again paused before the great place. He drew in a deep breath and said, "I want you to see it."

"I've seen it." This was exasperating. "Every fucking time we walk this way, I see it. Once and for all, I have seen it."

"I mean inside." His whisper was laden with the weight of crime. Guests were forbidden inside. Grounds to get the boot. And at that time, a woman inside was sacrilege.

He went to case the joint, to be sure it was empty. I waited on the corner until he came back for me.

We walked briskly up the path. I kept a lookout for passers-by while he opened the two doors. The first was padlocked. The second one opened by combination the way you open a vault. I tried peeking over his shoulder as he tumbled the numbers left and right and left, but could not see for myself. "This is hooked up to an echo chamber," he explained. "If anyone comes in, we'll hear them in plenty of time to hide you."

As if he'd muttered magic words, the second door eased open like one of the tales from *The Arabian Nights*.

I stepped onto a marble floor. At once, I took in high ceilings, mahogany moldings, dark, rich oil paintings in gilt frames, fireplaces, stairways long enough to reach the stars. Okay, so this was no tacky frat house.

He led me to a room where, on antique tabletops, on ornately carved shelves, on fireplace mantels, in every nook, were skulls. Human skulls. Each skull had a brass nameplate as if it were an endowed chair or a church pew dedicated in memory. These were luminary human remains, the skulls of once famous men.

"That's Cochese," he pointed out a skull in a glass tank pebbled with raw turquoise.

Skulls were the fruit of initiation. Retrieving the skull of a

64

deceased bigwig was ritual. The boys tapped were to bring back the skull of Aaron Burr or Cotton Mather or Boss Tweed.

I could've compared this to swallowing goldfish or twenty-two boys stuffing themselves into a phone booth, had the Skull and Bones boy not shown me some documents from a file cabinet. They were property deeds. Title to an island near Nova Scotia. Or maybe it was Nova Scotia. "Skull and Bones has more money than Yale." He detailed the corporate structure, listed assets, profit margins.

"You collect dividends even after you graduate?" I wanted to get this straight.

"No one graduates from Skull and Bones," he said. "This is a commitment forever. A marriage."

He put the documents away and told me how each member pledges to bequeath a hefty chunk of his personal estate back into the corporation. "After we die," he said. "And of course we leave our skulls here, too."

Because it takes money to make money, the boys tapped for Skull and Bones were the sons of enormously wealthy men. And a very select few who it was believed had potential to make a major killing on their own. There weren't many of those, though. It wasn't in the nature of Skull and Bones to gamble. These were not men who'd put everything on a roll of the dice.

I'd seen something like the sunken living room only in Maxfield Parrish paintings. Six Doric columns heralded the entrance. Plush chairs were arranged in a horseshoe. "This is where we have our rites of passage," he said. "Where we tell our life stories."

Each week the boys took seats around the one who sat in the center revealing himself, telling all. Not the stuff that gets listed in *Who's Who*, but secrets. Deep, dark, shameful secrets. Offhandedly, the Skull and Bones boy added, "We do it nude."

I was trying to absorb that tidbit when the combination lock echoed as if Death were coming. "I've got to hide you," he went pale, and we raced upstairs. In a small bedroom, he opened a closet and said, "Get in."

Hiding in a closet didn't appeal to me. The bed was a nicer place to wait. I sat down, drew my knees to my chin. My shoes left a mark where they slid against the velvet grain of the spread, and I pondered on Yalies stripping down to their skin, exposing themselves. What did they do afterwards? Step back into their boxer shorts? Zip up their flannel trousers? Casually button their Oxford shirts? Or did they stay naked? Frolic in imitation of English schoolboys at Eton?

Such musings gave me an idea. Reaching under my skirt, I wiggled out of my panties. Black silk panties. I put them on the nightstand next to a bronze ashtray adorned with a bronze skull. Then I took the ashtray and put it in my pocketbook.

The Skull and Bones boy called out to me, "All's clear," as he made his way up the steps. I came out from the bedroom and met up with him in the hall because I didn't want him to be the one to find my underwear.

Out on the street, around the corner, he stopped walking and said, "I wanted you to see it, to understand, because I want you to be my wife. I want to marry you."

Marry me? What kind of freak would want to marry me without knowing my body? Marry me? My skin started to itch, and I caught the last train out back to New York.

During the few weeks following, he called me often, wrote me letters, begged me to reconsider. Also, one of his friends called, worried about him, worried he was teetering off balance. I wondered if this friend were the one who found my panties.

In May, at the semester's end, I'd heard he'd gotten engaged to a girl who did her senior thesis on Emily Dickinson, and I thought: That is the end of that.

And it was the end of that except for two incidents: the first was a 5 A.M. phone call. "Who is this?" I asked, and a voice said, "We don't really do it nude." Next, the Skull and Bones boy showed up in New York, came banging at my door. I opened up, but I didn't invite him in. From across the threshold, he asked, "Why?"

"You never touched me," I told him. "All those nights, and you never did anything. You should've done something."

He sank to the floor. A plaintive wail escaped from the core of him. "I took you inside," he cried. "Inside Skull and Bones. I took you inside Skull and Bones."

I closed the door.

Slipping out of my robe, leaving it where it landed, I got back into my bed, back to the cute blue-eyed Marxist who hawked *The Daily Worker*. "Who was that?" he asked.

"Oh, nobody," I said. "Just some rich kid."

Guilty as Sin

I sit, leaning forward, exposing cleavage for the love of my life. "Tell me," I ask him, "what sins are you guilty of?"

Last night, the multimedia artist took me to yet another gallery opening. The second one in a week. Gallery openings, I've gathered, are the staple of his social diet. His appointment book is thick with their listings: Thurs., 6, Paula Cooper; Fri., 5:30, Stux; Sun., 3, Artist's Space. Like that. He goes only to the better ones, where the wine and cheese is quality, where the patrons have money to spend, where it is beneficial to be seen.

This show, the one he took me to last night at a West Broadway gallery, was titled *The Seven Deadly Sins*. As we moved from canvas to canvas, from the muck browns of *Sloth* to the red-and-pink swirls of *Lust*, the multimedia artist aimed to be a wit and asked, "Which sins are you guilty of?"

"All of them," I said.

"Yes," he agreed. "I suppose you are."

The love of my life, his eyes fixed on the swell of my breasts, claims to be guilty of no sins in particular. "I'm just guilty," he says. He doesn't explain why, but I know he is guilty of living on, living on in relative comfort, of not being dead. He runs a hand through his hair, which is drying out from age. Some of the silver strands stand away from his head. He should never have lived long enough to have his hair turn gray and brittle like that. "And you?" he asks me. "Do you experience guilt?"

Experiencing guilt is not at all the same thing as being guilty of sins. "No," I say. "I do not experience guilt." I feel sad about things like people living on the street, famines, wars, calves raised in boxes for veal. I wish such things were not so, but I do not feel guilty about them.

This is not to say I've never experienced guilt. I have. Things I've felt guilty about are: 1) The *A* I got in Statistics. Statistics was not a subject I had an aptitude for. The professor, a sorry man whose underwear band rose up over his pants, developed a serious crush on me, so I set forth a proposition. I was hoping to get a *B–* from the deal, but he gave me an *A*. I didn't deserve an *A*. Not for any of it. 2) When I kill bugs, insects, I experience guilt. I kill them because I don't want them near me. But I believe it's wrong to take a life simply because it's pesky.

That is the complete list of things I feel guilty about. Except, of course, the guilt I experience over not experiencing guilt. Like after spending the day with the hit man, I'll go home, kiss my husband, mouth to mouth, have conversation and dinner with him, and think nothing of it, as if I'd spent the day window-shopping or lunching with the Kessel sisters as opposed to lunching on another man's cock. Sometimes, on those days, I step out of myself and ask: Shouldn't I feel guilty?

I ask the same thing when I buy expensive, useless trinkets, eat dessert with extra whipped cream, or when I swear to the hit man I have sex only with him.

That I'm essentially guilt-free is further evidence of my heritage hosed down, lost. The way the Yiddish language was not passed along to me, nor a taste for gefilte fish, nor a recipe for poppyseed cookies, nor a pair of Sabbath candlesticks, Jewish guilt got tossed out, too.

From hearsay, I know Jews are supposed to experience fabulous guilt. It's in the blood, the genes, the traditions. Supposedly, we invented guilt. The same day we came up with monotheism, we discovered we weren't perfect. Our Messiah hasn't come because we don't deserve Him. We don't call our mothers daily, we didn't get straight A pluses in school, we don't always clean up after ourselves, we didn't die when so many others did.

Jewish sins are sins of omission. It's not what we do that's so bad. It's what we don't do. And while I will go as far as to regret a missed opportunity, regret isn't guilt, and passing up a ménage à trois is not a sin of omission.

Perhaps there is another brand of guilt I can attach to myself. Later, at home, I call up the hit man and ask him, "Is there such a thing as Catholic guilt?"

"You can't be serious." He's flabbergasted at my ignorance. "Catholics invented guilt."

"I thought Jews did," I say.

"Well, yeah but..." He dismisses Jewish guilt as piddling, small potatoes. "Catholics perfected it," he says. "We got the patent. Guilt torments us whenever we have a good time. Especially a good time centered around our cocks. Like God gave men cocks to trip us up. Guilt if you think about your cock. More guilt if you touch it, even accidentally. And if a girl touches it for you, you might as well kiss it good-bye. Except the thought of kissing it costs you two Hail Marys, two Our Fathers, and an Act of Contrition. See, we got guilt down to a business. We pay. For quality and quantity. We got to keep track of our sins, the particulars. Let's say I go to confession, admit to touching my cock five times, and I receive absolution. I go home and remember, Shit! I forgot to mention that sixth time, in the shower, when I rubbed it with soap. Now I'm damned for eternity."

"But you get to confess," I note. "Absolution frees you from guilt."

"And how long," the hit man asks, "do you think a state of grace lasts? You're not out the church door before you have another filthy thought. Besides, no one comes completely clean in confession. We tell lies there." He stops talking, abruptly.

I sense a change in mood, tone. Suspicion washes over his voice the way a shade comes down. "Why are you asking this?" He wants to know, "Where have you been? I haven't seen you for days. You feel guilty about something? You got a confession to make?"

"No," I say. "I don't feel guilty. I don't feel guilty about anything. Nothing at all."

Here I am, a left-handed woman, Jewish, married, a believer in God, committing sins. Deadly sins, mortal sins, venial sins. I have broken seven of the Ten Commandments. Yet God has not extended a long arm down from the heavens to bat me across the mouth. My guts don't wrench, my conscience doesn't pang. Guilt does not prey upon me. My sleep is that of the innocent.

"You know," the hit man has another thought, "the funny thing about all this is the saints, the saints were sinners. Yeah, the saints, they sinned big."

The Only Son

he way he's barged into my life, the hit man enters the Café Dante. His black fedora is pulled down low. He wears an overcoat, black leather gloves, and he does not need to look, to scan the room to find me. He knows exactly where I'm sitting. He comes directly to my table and pulls out a chair, the same chair his mother vacated only a moment before.

"You haven't been waiting long, have you?" he asks. He is always on time, and I, too, make a point of punctuality because if I'm even five minutes late, he wants to know why.

"I got here early," I tell him. "About an hour ago."

"So what have you been doing?" he asks.

The hit man's mother has been dead for a lot of years, so I expect him to scoff when I answer, "Your mother was here." From the other side she came to speak her piece.

He doesn't scoff. He doesn't say anything, and I ask, "What's a *puttana*?"

His hand goes to his cheek, his mouth falls open. "My mother called you that? My mother called you a *puttana*? That's the worst thing you can call a woman. Why did she call you that? What else did she say?"

Before I can begin to tell him, he signals me to halt. "Wait," he says. "From the beginning. What went on here?"

It went like this: I was sitting here, drinking my coffee, minding my own business when there she was, materialized in the chair across from me. Steely-eyed, her hair grey, she wore a black dress. Although I didn't have a view of her from below the tabletop, I knew her black stockings were rolled to her knees. There was no mistaking her for anyone else. I'd seen her picture, a studio portrait in a gold frame, on the hit man's desk. Also, pinned to her dress was the garnet brooch I have on, the one the hit man gave me. "This was my mother's," he'd said. "She'd have wanted me to give it to you."

"That's mine," she spied it right away. "Where'd you get that? My husband give me that." She reached across the table to snatch back her circle of garnets pinned to my collar.

"Your son gave it to me," I told her. "He said you'd have wanted me to have it."

"Well, I don't want you to have it," but she let it go, gave it up and said, "Ah, you got him so twisted in knots. He's gaga. You think I don't know? I know. I see what goes on. I see how you got him. I see how he cooks for you. My recipes he cooks for you. That's not right, a man cooking for you. I didn't raise my only son to cook dinner for some *puttana*. What's the matter, you don't know how to cook a meal?"

"I can cook."

"Oh yeah?" she challenged. "So tell me, what do you cook for that husband of yours?"

Her knowledge of my husband, that I have a husband, led me to assume that I couldn't get away with a lie. "Frozen dinners," I admitted.

"Frozen dinners," she repeated, shook her head sadly. "And how many years you been married?"

"Four," I said.

"Four years your husband's been eating nothing but frozen foods? He puts up with that?"

"We go out to eat a lot," I explained. "To restaurants."

"Four years and the man hasn't had a home-cooked meal. And four years married and no children. How come you got no children? Your womb as shriveled as your heart? Is that it?"

"There is such a thing as birth control," I told her. "I don't have to go drop a kid every year if I don't want to."

"Hey," her nostrils flared, "don't talk to me like I'm Irish. No one said anything about acting Irish here. Those Scaramouch, thirteen, fourteen kids and kissing the priest's ass. But two, three children. A family. It's not natural to be the way you are. What's the matter? You don't got time to be a mother? Too busy painting your face and shaving your armpits?"

"You too with the shaved armpits?" I asked. "What is that? A family hang-up?"

Although the hit man likes that I wear makeup and perfume to linger on his sheets after I've gone, he wishes, has requested even, I not shave under my arms. But I have not complied. I continue to shave, and he has continued to nuzzle there, to wipe away a trickle of sweat with his finger, to bring his finger to his nose to sniff, to his mouth to taste, the way a teenage boy does after getting a finger up his first girl.

"No more bullshit," the hit man's mother dispensed with small talk. "I want you to stay away from my son. He don't know how to handle you. He's sensitive. Takes after his father. Mush."

"He's a grown man," I reminded her. "Quite capable of taking care of himself. He doesn't need his mother looking out for him," I said. "He's tough."

"Tough?" she snorted. "Tough? He don't even carry a gun. Tough, hah! You could hurt him. You're no good."

"I'm good," I said, genuinely bothered at the aspersion cast. "I'm a good person," but I lacked the conviction such a statement ought to have carried because how much, and exactly what, did she know? On which occasions was she watching over me?

"He needs a good woman," she said. "Not some *puttana*. I'm telling you, you stay away from my son."

"And what if I don't?" I am capable of a strong will, although it wasn't easy staring down a ghost. She was able to be far more elusive than I could ever be as long as I'm on this earth, among the living.

"I could make your life hell," she warned.

Yes, she could indeed make my life difficult, like a dybbuk from my faith, creating havoc for the sport of it, tricks only the dead can play. Aiming to cut a deal, I said, "You know it could be worse. He could do worse than me. He is a man ripe for a lamia, a spirit who seduces dreaming men, men who are dreamers, men like your son. Given that alternative, I'm not so bad. Besides, do you realize how miserable he'd be if I were to leave him?"

"You're going to leave him someday. Why wait?" She, this ghost, knew things about the future.

"Because until then, I make him happy. He does love me, you know."

"Love," she grimaced.

"Love," I said. "True love. He's found that. He has it. He has it for me. Whatever I might be, he loves me. How many of us," I asked her, "in our lifetimes, get to find love?" I was referring to her. Romantic love, I knew, was not something she got to have. The hit man had told me how he was four months in her womb before his father did the right thing by marrying her, a woman he didn't love. And perhaps I was talking about myself, too. "Don't deny him love," I said.

Before fading away, she accepted my terms, came to an understanding with me. After all, we, she and I, are very much alike: stubborn, calculating, and toying with the fate of her only son.

"From the beginning," he says. "What went on here?"

Separate Bags

*T*he middle Kessel sister and I, having agreed it was time, meet in Grand Central Station, beneath the ceiling of the constellations, by the ticket windows.

Both of us carry white paper bags—a container of coffee, a muffin. Sustenance for the journey, nourishment for the quest.

Our train is destined for outlying regions, other worlds. We are going to the suburbs, to the Junior League Thrift Store in search of dead people's clothes.

The conductor, who looks too young to be wearing a uniform of any kind, punches our tickets, and the Kessel sister asks me a question. "Do you think if we were rich, really rich, we'd still do this?"

I don't have to consider the question to answer. "Yes. Absolutely," I say. "The money is irrelevant."

I discovered my affinity for dead people's clothes when I was a student, short on cash but long on affection for lovely things, good fabrics, elegant cuts. Not only were dead people's clothes affordable to me, but such clothes flattered my shape and my sensibilities. Dead people's clothes have wonderful smells to them—sachets, cigarette smoke, perfumes faded save for a hint. Also, they have histories attached and allow me to wonder if the lace flapper dress danced on speakeasy tabletops, what sort of men fingered the fringes of the embroidered shawl, did the satin pumps walk home alone in the rain? I have come to understand this: Things survive people. The outfit lasts longer than the love affair.

"There's nothing like it, is there?" the Kessel sister says. "The way the adrenaline pumps from unearthing a beaded cashmere sweater, a 50¢ tag stapled to the sleeve." She compares such a find to an archaeological dig, the discovery of a pottery shard having value way beyond the monetary.

The view from the train window moves from burned-out buildings to warehouses, factories, and our conversation moves along, too. "For the third time this week," the Kessel sister says, "I dreamed I drove my car off a bridge. Which is pretty spooky considering I don't even drive."

"Dreams," I smile mischievously, baiting her. "Don't talk to me about dreams."

The middle Kessel sister is a dream fan, gets off on analyzing them, poking around psyches, uncovering the subconscious. "You had a juicy one, didn't you?" She'd kill to hear it.

"You bet," I taunt her. "Very juicy."

"Tell me, tell me," she bounces on the seat, pummels at the armrest.

It went like this: I was in a forest. A dark forest, although it wasn't night. I was naked except for a cape that clasped at the neck but swung open. In my right hand I carried a basket filled with flower petals, the same as a flower girl at a wedding carries. With my left hand, I tossed the petals hither and yonder, like an idiot. Suddenly, as only in dreams, the trees metamorphosed into cocks. Enormous cocks towering over me. Then, I

81

looked down, and all the toadstools were eensy-teensy cocks underfoot. I was worried I'd step on one and mush it. The atmosphere aroused me, and I attempted to mount a tree-penis, the biggest one, the giant redwood of cocks. But to no avail. Next, I squatted over one of the toadstools, but it was way too small. From tree-penis to fungus-cock, I darted, hoping one would fit. But none did, and I started screaming, "There must be a way. There must be a way." That's when I woke up.

The Kessel sister is staring at me, and I ask her, "So, what do you think?"

"I'm starving," she gets her muffin from the white paper bag. "Ravenous," she bites into it.

There are methods, rules, guidelines to thrift store shopping. Most effective is to be Machiavellian: divide and conquer. The Kessel sister takes *Skirts*. I go to *Jackets*.

Flipping through a motley lot of drab tweeds, corduroys, and velveteens, a snippet of fabric two racks over beckons me. Drawn to the colors—pink, orange, brilliant blues, vivid green—I go to it. It's one of those Hawaiian shirts patterned in tropical fruit—mango, papaya, pineapples. Scrumptious! Delectable right down to the wooden buttons that resemble coconut shells.

This is too delightful an item to put back on the rack, but even if I would wear such a happy shirt, it is yards too big for me.

I decide to buy it for the hit man, and having taken that step, I go look for a tie for the multimedia artist. That tie he wore to the 57th Street gallery was of man-made fibers and soiled. "What do you think of my tie?" he'd asked, lifting it as if I wanted a closer look. "It's the only one I've got," he said.

The tie rack at the Junior League Thrift Store spins like a playground roundabout offering a cacophony of ties. I pick through them, refusing the ones spotted with food stains, with frayed edges, with fabric too grotesque to touch. I settle on two:

a heavy maroon silk, and a teal blue decorated with silver art deco bubbles.

My husband is not a man who would wear a shirt of many fruits or a bubbled tie. In general, dead people's clothes disturb him. He insists my purchases be dry-cleaned before I hang them in the closet. But given that I'm buying gifts for the hit man and the multimedia artist, it'd be immoral to return to my husband empty-handed, with nothing.

I do not even toy with the idea of looking for a gift here for the love of my life. In a store filled with dead people's things, I'd run the risk of buying him something that was once his own.

The ship made entirely from clam shells and pipe cleaners would not charm my husband. Nor would he like to have a coffee mug—Elmsford Volunteer Fire Department embossed in gold—with a broken handle. He'd take one look at the orange ashtray from a defunct Playboy Club and ask, "Why did you buy this?" and I wouldn't want to tell him, "Because I didn't want to leave you out."

It's good, then, that I find the 1953 Rand McNally Atlas, leather-bound and in decent shape. Providing there are no silverfish multiplying in the pages, he'll enjoy this. My husband likes maps.

At the counter, I arrange my goods, lay them out. "These things are all yours?" the cashier asks me. Pinned to her coral smock is a tag that reads: Volunteer.

"Yes, all mine," I tell her. "I'm paying for them together, but could you put them in three separate bags?"

I wait outside for the middle Kessel sister. She comes along with two overstuffed shopping bags, eyes my skimpy purchases, and asks, "That's all you got? Do you feel okay?"

I assure her I'm fine, and we go to a diner for coffee.

We sit in a booth, and the Kessel sister tells me, "I bought three coats. What am I going to do with three coats?"

I suggest the obvious. She could give one to each of her sisters, but the middle Kessel sister is possessive of her dead people's clothes, and talks herself into holding on to them. "Who knows, we might get one of those frigid days, and one coat won't be warm enough."

I agree, you never know how cold it can get, and I tell her we've got to hurry if we want to make our train. She pays for our coffee, I leave a tip, and we get to the station just as our train arrives.

It isn't until after we're seated and the train pulls away that I remember I left my three bags in the diner, in the booth, and although I ought to be aggravated, I find I am glad to be rid of things to carry.

Keeping Track

*M*y mother is on the phone, calling to tell me about the unveiling for my great-aunt Lila. Lila was from my father's side of the family. In some ways my mother keeps up with my father's family as if she were your everyday widow. She attends their weddings and funerals and invites them to dinner once a year.

I have never been to the unveiling of a headstone. Nor to a funeral. When, on different days, years apart, my grandmothers died, my mother said I was too young to go to such depressing things. My grandfathers were both dead before I was born. One way or another, the men in my family don't stick around for long.

If such ceremonies—funeral and unveiling—were held for my father, they were kept secret from me. The only event marking my father's death was the two FBI agents at our door, like Gabriel and Michael, coming to tell us my father went out a window. Then they wanted to snoop around our house, nose through his belongings. Only we had none of his belongings. My mother had thrown them all away, as if he never existed.

Of course, the only way I knew he was alive to begin with was because, once every year or so, he sent me a postcard from the Golden Nugget, pictures of slot machines and roulette wheels, like my father was James Bond.

I imagine an unveiling to be an event with flourish, fanfare, the way an artist unveils a masterpiece, pulling away a sheet— ta-dum! "So, how was it?" I ask my mother.

"How was it? It was barbaric." My mother does not wish to remember the dead. Her motto is, "Out of life, out of mind."

"Could you hold on a second?" I ask her, and I put down the phone, locate cigarettes, matches, ashtray. "I'm back," I say, and my mother says, "I wish you wouldn't smoke. It's so unattractive."

I took my first cigarette when I was fifteen. After dinner—ham fillets, canned corn, mashed potatoes from boxed flakes—I lit up. "You're making a dreadful mistake," my mother warned. I thought she was going to go on about health risks, how smoking would tar my lungs, wreck my heart and vascular system. Instead she said, "Boys won't like kissing you with tobacco on your breath."

Wanting to learn more about great-aunt Lila's unveiling, I ask for details. What went on, exactly? What tributes were spoken? Did anyone weep? How much is remembered of a person dead for a year?

"It was morbid," my mother says. "Everyone talking about her as if she were alive, as if they had lunch with her yesterday."

I, too, have a vivid memory of great-aunt Lila. For my ninth birthday she gave me *The Diary of Anne Frank*.

After the party, when all the guests had gone, my mother took the book from my pile of loot, showed it to her boyfriend, the dufus who would become my stepfather, and she said, "Do you believe that kike Lila? Buying her this?"

Less than a year later, my mother was able to divorce my father on the grounds that he'd deserted her. After that, she quit inviting great-aunt Lila, along with the rest of his family, to my birthday parties.

For no reason other than what was off-limits was too tempting to resist, I retrieved *The Diary of Anne Frank* from the closet where my mother had hidden it. Far too modern to outright ban a book, my mother said, "You're not going to enjoy that. You won't identify with the main character." In hopes I'd identify with main characters, I was raised on *Eloise, Nancy Drew, The Five Little Peppers*.

In one sitting, without getting up for so much as a bathroom break, I read *The Diary of Anne Frank*. When I finished the book, I was a changed person in two ways: 1) I became aware, having identified with the main character after all, of what could've happened, happened to me. 2) I developed a taste for Nazi atrocity stories.

At night, in bed, under the covers, I propped books up on bent knees, held a flashlight on the pages, and read *Treblinka, Judgment at Nuremberg, The War against the Jews*. I read, and reread, the grotesque passages, the lurid descriptions of babies used as clay pigeons for skeet shooting, of experiments on twins, of women—heads shaved, gold teeth extracted, naked—lined up for the euphemistic shower. I devoured the recountings of torture, of degradation, the systematic stripping away of dignity, humanity, life.

Each night, in the moments between dog-earing the page to mark my place and falling asleep, I asked myself this question: How would I have survived?

If children don't know the theory of natural selection verbatim, they do know it by instinct. The strong make it. The weak get picked on. Every child, in a panic to gain a prominent position in the neighborhood pecking order, climbs onto and over smaller, softer heads. I was quite familiar with the sound of spir-

87

it crunching under my P.F. Flyers. But the other? How would I have survived that?

The scenario I came up with was this: I'd have joined a resistance movement, lived in the forest, foraged nuts and berries to eat, worn a beret. We, my compatriots and I, having planned and executed raids, would then disappear back behind the trees where, by moonlight, I'd have sex with our leader who would be French and gorgeous.

That was a scenario I liked. However, it wasn't a probable one. Rather, I'd have tried to fuck my way out of such a predicament. Aimed to have caught the commandant's fancy, his roving eye. I would've been a Nazi's whore, sucked his dick, saved my ass like that.

Obviously, this is moot. My mother was accurate in her assessment. I have not, and most likely will not, face the evil, the event that would require great strength to survive, the event to define my existence. However, this does not diminish the need to be remembered. If anything, without a defining event, the chances of being remembered decrease.

There ought to be unveilings for the living because people can be forgotten as easily as packages can be left behind in a booth in a diner. We need a day to remember our past, a day to think of all our lovers, to give testimony as to how it was pushing, sweating, grinding, until—like stone set against the surf—it wore down to nothing. I would like a day to think of them all because if I forget them, they could forget me.

I can, at the drop of a hat, recall every detail of my first fuck, even though with hindsight and experience, I know it was bland. Still, it was the first. Regardless of how many partners, positions, places I've been in, with, my virginity got lost only one time.

People try and fib about that, claim virginity on two or more occasions. A girl in my high school—left back twice, wore stockings with runs in them as if it were 1959 and she were leader of a girl gang—banged half the senior class and the shop teacher. Yet, one day in the girls' room, when I'd asked for some tips, an information exchange, a dialogue, she fingered the gold cross around her neck and said, "I'm a virgin."

You can say what you want, but the fact remains: virginity is a one-shot deal.

However, you can have more than one virgin, if you'd want to. A virgin boy pops off on contact. I know so because I've had three of them intact: 1) A boy on the college soccer team, the goalie. 2) The sixteen-year-old kid who lived with his parents in the apartment below mine. I had to. He was adorable. 3) A *mitzvah*. A good deed, a kindness for a gawky computer genius in desperate straits.

From my end, their first times weren't anything to write about in my diary. Yet, even considering the cruddy sex, the dick without discipline, I'd have a go with a virgin again anytime. With a virgin, I get remembered. Maybe not in a way as formal as an unveiling. The tribute to me isn't an organized memorial service. But I do know somewhere, someplace, are three men who, now and again, stop whatever they're doing—mowing the lawn, designing a program, fucking a professor's wife—to pause, to think of me, to remember me.

Beginning with
Jealous Greek Goddesses

*T*he multimedia artist is engaged in an extended phone conversation. It's remarkably rude of him to yak away while I'm here, but I welcome the reprieve and take the opportunity to snoop around.

On his dresser top is a pair of earrings. Hammered brass disks. Made in India. No doubt purchased from a street vendor. Five bucks tops. These are not my earrings.

Another thing about these earrings: They were placed here deliberately. It was intended I discover them, because not one item—not a paper clip—in this immense loft is otherwise out of place. His books, records, CDs, thousands of each, are arranged on shelves by category, author, performer. Coded, like in a library. But unlike a library, tacked to his shelves are notes which read: *Not for Borrowing*.

The earrings on his dresser also have a message attached. Although not written down, nor tacked up, it is loud and clear. It reads: I have another lover besides you.

I picture this woman who wears brass earrings. I see her this way: shapeless dress, mouse-colored hair in need of styling, Birkenstock sandals on her feet, carrying a nylon backpack in lieu of a purse.

Next, it occurs to me perhaps these earrings weren't left here by a woman. Perhaps the multimedia artist bought the earrings himself and put them in a place where I was likely to spot them. A sorry attempt to even the score, and a possible one, except I can't see him springing for the five bucks. Had he concocted such a scheme, I'd have discovered something other than earrings. Something with a 19¢ price tag. A bobby pin or a tampon. Therefore, I return to my original conclusion: He is getting laid on the side.

Despite my own entanglements, I have the gall to expect fidelity. How dare I make such a demand? I rationalize it this way: I'm like a lioness with cubs. More than one cub. Three cubs. Maybe four, but my cubs have only me to provide for them. I lick them clean. I protect them from predators, stand guard, bare my fangs, snarl, snap at whomever approaches. They are mine. I won't give up any one of them.

Yet here is the multimedia artist aiming to rub my nose in what might've taken place on another night. I wait for my territorial hackles to rise. But they don't rise. I don't seem to be bothered. I am not in a snit. I have no desire, no need, to scoop up these earrings, march over, and fling them in his face.

It had been my habit, for several years, to write letters expressing my devotion to the love of my life. I would hand-deliver these letters, perfumed and sealed with wax, to his mailbox.

One afternoon, as I dropped a letter off, I spied a package, gift-wrapped in blue paper, a card taped to the box, his name written across the envelope in neat script. A script my left hand could never master. I gaped at this box, fury engulfing me like a fireball. A rage, worthy of Medea, came on. Who was this bitch daring to bring gifts to my beloved?

I took it. I lifted the box, slipped it under my jacket, kept it in place by holding my lapels up as if against the cold.

Like the thief I was, I raced home, locked myself inside. Hands trembling, I ripped the paper away to expose a box of pecan log rolls. Caramel and nut candy sold in gas stations throughout the south. I felt smug. I'd never buy him such unappetizing candy, candy that resembled fat, speckled fingers, purchased at an Esso station.

I put water up to boil. It was my intention to steam open the envelope, only it got scorched, charred on the flame. What's done was done, so I tore it open. In that same schoolgirl script was written: Picked these up for you on our trip to Charleston. Enjoy! Fondly, Marjorie and Steve.

I tried to smooth out the blue wrapping paper, which proved to be like putting Humpty-Dumpty together again. I could've simply thrown the evidence—card, paper, candy—away, except I kept imagining Marjorie and Steve waiting for an expression of gratitude, a mere thank you, which would not materialize if I threw their gift in the trash.

I slid the note into the burned envelope, took the wadded ball of paper along with the box of candy, went to his apartment, and knocked on the door. "Pecan log rolls," I handed him the whole mess. "From Marjorie and Steve."

Irrationalities, jealousies, are part and parcel to passion, to sex, to love. This is evidenced by a long literary tradition beginning with jealous Greek goddesses. Yet when confronted with the brass earrings, concrete evidence of betrayal, no jealousy surfaces. All I can muster is a smirk.

I toy with this plan: Swap earrings. Leave my pearl drops on the dresser, wear the hammered brass disks home. She, the other woman, would be getting the better half of that bargain. As if something magical happened, she could leave behind tacky brass earrings and have them turn into pearls.

That generous I am not. I'd have given her my earrings gladly, but not the rest, the wonderful part.

I scurry back to the bed as the multimedia artist returns from his phone call. "Sorry I took so long," he says. "That was a friend, and I couldn't hang up on *her. She* had to talk with me about *something.*" His plea is desperate, obvious, and I give him what he wants because what harm can it do to feign indignation? "Oh, really?" I huff. "And are those *her* earrings on your dresser?"

He lights up! Twinkles from the electricity I've generated. Oh, how he shines that I care enough to be jealous.

Another Crime of Passion

The night is balmy. Bizarre for this time of year. Treetops sway gently. Purple clouds billow across the sky like a setting for a dream.

"It's like Indian summer," the hit man remarks.

"Global warming," is my take. I don't want to be here, out on the streets, walking. I wanted to stay indoors, inside the hit man's apartment, insular.

Many couples are out strolling, hand in hand, spooning as if it were really spring instead of a fluke warm front. In darkened corners and doorways, people kiss. We pass a pair dry humping against the hood of a car. "Isn't that nice?" the hit man says. "Love. The expressions of love." This is a dig at me. While we walk, I won't hold his hand, refuse to let him slide an arm around my waist.

He claims to understand, to follow the logic whereby married women can't engage in public displays of affection with men other than their husbands. But still, not one to give up easily, he tries to pull a fast one. On the pretense of guiding me, steering me across the street, he takes me by the elbow. I pull away, shake free of his grasp, but as he brings his hand back to his side, it brushes at my butt, lingers there.

"Cut that out," I say.

"I'm sorry. I can't help myself. I can't let go of the fantasy," he tells me. "You know, you and me, we're just Mr. and Mrs. Smith out for a walk. So, what's wrong with that?"

"Everything is wrong with that. It's impossible."

Turning the corner onto 12th Street, we pass by some babe in a low, a very low, cut blouse. Her jacket is open. Her breasts are big and spill over. The fact of the matter is, big boobs flashing or not, the woman is homely. Her face is horsey, her hair limp, her thighs rub, chafe together, and her eyes admit defeat.

Yet the hit man turns for a doubletake.

On this occasion, my ire is for real. I am jealous, not of her, that homely woman, but of the attention the hit man pays her. To convey my disgruntlement, I jab him in the stomach. Not hard, but with enough force to remind him I am here.

He stops in his tracks, stands still, and lets out a laugh. A belly laugh, deep, genuine, an explosion of joy. What is it with these men, my men, that my declarations of jealousy should tickle them so? Perhaps they mistake them for declarations of love.

Since taking up with the hit man, he's been after me to say *I love you.* In a singsong voice, he has cajoled, "I know you do. You might as well admit it." He has dared me, "What are you afraid of?" And in the midst of sex, he has gripped my arms and demanded, "Tell me. Tell me you love me."

But I'm on my toes. I avoid such traps.

One night, in his bed, with me at his side, he stared up at the ceiling and had this to say: "I imagine I'm on my death bed. I'm about to cross over to the other side. You're here with me, and the priest has come to give last rites. But I don't want any last rites. I tell the priest to fuck off. What I want is for you to tell me you love me. From your lips, I want to hear that before I go. But you just stand there looking down at me. My mouth goes dry. Still, I manage to croak out, 'Please, tell me,' with my last breath. Then, that's it. I'm dead, and you lean in close over my corpse and whisper, 'I love you.'"

"I would never do that," I told him. "I would never say *I love you* to a dead man."

"So you'll tell me before I'm dead?" He clung to his hope.

I placed my hand softly on his cheek, let it rest there, and said, "No. It doesn't mean that."

That I have responded, demonstrated displeasure at him for eyeballing that sad woman's bosoms, causes his heart to soar, makes his world light, and he trusts enough to confess, "You know, I only looked to see what you'd do."

I might doubt another man's word on that, but not his. I nod and say, "I know."

We walk another block, and again he stops. He takes me by the shoulders, spins me so I face him, so he can look me square in the eye. He's big on eye contact, which unsettles me. "Listen," he says. "Listen to me. Don't retaliate, okay?"

"Retaliate?"

"Yeah, retaliate. Get even," he says as if he were translating, as if *retaliate* were another language or a custom of foreign people. "Please, promise me. Promise you won't look at another man just to even the score."

Perhaps *retaliate* is another language, custom. One of his people and not mine. But rather than admit the thought hadn't occurred to me, that I had no intention of retaliating, I let him go on, talk more. I want to see where he's headed.

"I wouldn't be able to take it," he says. "Please. I'm begging you. Don't do it. I'm serious. The thought of you looking at another man, it'd make me go crazy. Push me over the edge. If you so much as glanced at some man and I saw you, I don't know what I'd do. I wouldn't be responsible."

Again, I take him at his word.

"People like us," he says, "we could be driven to commit crimes of passion."

An Eye for What Looks Good

*I*t's an unpleasant discovery. The multimedia artist owns more than one pair of clogs. Besides the ones on his feet, a second pair is resting, like old men's slippers, by the bed. I try to ignore them, look elsewhere, scan book shelves, take a gander at the new artwork, until he calls for my attention. "Well," his arms akimbo, he asks, "what do you think?"

"About what?"

"My new shirt," he says.

It's true. He's wearing a new shirt. A spanking-new T-shirt. Yellow, with the letters NYU spelled out in purple. Over the T-shirt, he has on suspenders, black with yellow diamond patterns. From the folds, I know they, too, are new, fresh from the box. "And my braces," he adds.

"Braces?" To me, braces are what kids wear on their teeth or polio victims on matchstick legs. A correctional device.

"Yes, braces." He hooks his thumbs under the suspenders like a yokel. "I went shopping yesterday. I got many new things."

Something's up. He's not a man anyone would peg a clothes-horse. Almost exclusively he wears paint-stained jeans, ratty sweatshirts, and those clogs. Often, his underwear has holes in it.

I used to concern myself with how men dressed. I would take them on shopping expeditions, rearrange their wardrobes, give them style, panache. I have an eye for what looks good, an instinct for which men belong in tweeds, which men fit classically into Levi's, and who can pull off an Armani suit. But I've lost what little inclination I had left to lend my services. Let them wear what they want.

The multimedia artist is bent on showing me his purchases, the new clothes he has bought for himself. He goes to his closet, and I crane my neck scouting for a shoe rack. A third pair of clogs is on the closet floor, and I wonder if he bought clogs in bulk, if he shoe-shopped the way Imelda Marcos did, if, at once, he bought up all the clogs in the store, the city, the world.

Emerging from his closet with three shirts on wire hangers, his face is pink, sweet like cotton candy. I think of Gatsby bringing out stacks of silk shirts, displaying them as if they were works of art. Gatsby's shirts were beautiful shirts, but still the episode was embarrassing. The multimedia artist's shirts are hideous. He holds them out, fans them, as if he were a salesman trying to interest me in something I'd never buy. They look like girl's shirts, although not shirts I'd wear. Two of them are navy blue, one is trimmed with a maroon braid. The third shirt is white and has doodads stitched to the collar. Bugle beads, maybe. "Well?" he asks.

"Well what?" My evasiveness is ridiculous.

"Come on," he insists I give my opinion. He waits for me to say the shirts are nice. That's all he wants from me, to say something simple, something reassuring, that I like the shirts. With each long second, he and his shirts grow more pathetic, expanding sadly with my inability to say, "Nice. Very nice."

I can't explain why such words won't take shape. It's not that I am above a lie. At this moment, I could easily tell another lie. With no difficulty at all, I could say to him, "I'm falling in love with you." A lie of such grand proportions would glide off my tongue. But this small lie, a white lie, that his shirts are fine shirts, is a lie I can't bring myself to tell.

Mary Magdalene and Company

*I*t's a ploy, another sneaky attempt to get us out in the world where we can be seen, witnessed, as if public outings were the same as posting banns. And I must give credit where it's due. It's clever of him asking me to take a day, a full day, and go with him to the track. To Belmont, to the Meadowlands, to Yonkers, whichever, to place bets—daily doubles, exactas, trifectas, perfectas, quinellas—to sit in the stands with all the other people, to root for horses called Shiloh Storm, Arabella, Homer's Odyssey. The hit man is betting on the genetic factor, that inherently I won't be able to resist the call of the ponies. "Look," I try to explain, and hardly for the first time, "going to the track sounds like a perfectly lovely way to spend a day, but it's got nothing on staying here, the two of us alone, private."

"You never want to go out with me anymore," he says, and he is right.

"It's a matter of priorities," I tell him. "We can't have everything, so I do what I like best."

"Why can't we have everything? Why can't we have it all?

There's nothing in that marriage for you. That is," his voice ices over with suspicion, "if it's what you say it is."

"Don't talk to me like that," I warn. "If you think I'm lying, then I'll leave right now."

"Okay, okay," he backs down, hands positioned in surrender. "I believe you. It's just so frustrating. You know, we are so right together." He waits for me to concur, as if we were something nature created to ensure the other's survival, like bumblebees and clover. But I don't concur, so he locates another angle. "I know this place is too small for the two of us, but I can get us a bigger place. I'll put the word out on the street we're after what, a loft? A big one-bedroom in Chelsea? Or you want to go further downtown? I know people who can help us out."

He expects me to be impressed by his contacts, this anonymous network of Sicilians who do favors for other Sicilians. I might admit to a slight charge, but hardly enough to shake me. "The size of this place is irrelevant," I say, but before he can presume I'd live with him anywhere, I add, "Even if you got us the fucking Taj Mahal, I wouldn't live with you."

"That's not what you said before."

"What? What did I say before?"

"Many times," he says, "you indicate you're happy with me." He's got dates and direct quotes handy. What he's done is sift through all my words panning for gold, for nuggets, flakes, dust, to save, treasure, bank on. "Like the sex. Last Saturday you said this was the best sex you ever had in your life. Right here. With me." This is what he saves, things said in bed, utterances of the moment, as valuable as iron pyrite and meant to last as long as the orgasm that prompted them.

"Pillow talk," I say.

"So, it's all crap? Lies? Is that what you're telling me?" He musters the strength of a bully and makes threats. "You've got to decide. Here and now. I'm not going to be your mistress anymore."

"Mistress!" I laugh. "You? A mistress wears filmy *peignoirs*, feather boas, has Zsa Zsa Gabor hair."

"Okay, okay," he concedes the humor. "Whatever you want to call it. I don't want it anymore. I want you. With me. At the end of the day, I want to come home and find you here. In the morning, I want to watch you sleep. So, what's it going to be?"

"No."

"No? No what? What's no?"

"No," I say. "I will not live with you."

"Then it's over between us."

"If that's how you want it," I call his bluff and head for the door. His face explodes into raw fear, and he holds me back. "This isn't how I want it. Things got away from us here. Really, how did this start? I wanted us to have a day, go to the track, fun, light. It's this place, babe." He turns his head slowly, taking in his apartment. "I need to get out more."

"Get out on your own time," I tell him. "Not on my time. Our time," I cover myself. "Our time is best spent here." I move closer to him and say, "Right this minute, you've got a choice. We can go out, have a drink, hear some music, jazz even. Or, we can stay here, and I'll run my tongue from your eyes to your ankles and back again. So, go on. Pick." I slide my hand along his thigh, fingernails scraping lightly to let him know this: There's no choice.

"I get it," he says. "Everything's clear to me now. It all makes sense. You're a whore. *Puttana*." He calls me the same thing his mother called me. The family curse.

I shrug. I don't mind being called a whore. For one thing, there's some truth to it. Also, there are worse things a person could be.

103

Once, in a cruel moment, the love of my life said to me, "Sometimes, I think you're a snake. Not an exotic snake. Not a cobra or a python. Just a common-variety garden snake. A brief chase and you're easily enough caught. Still, you'll never get warmer than room temperature."

Unlike that comment, which did wound me, the hit man's dart missed its mark. Aware of this, he says, as if it were news to him, "I'm in love with a whore." He shakes his head. "I do love you," he says. "In spite of it."

"Oh no, my sweet," I set him straight, "you love me not in spite of, but *because* of. You love me *because* I am a whore."

It's an old, old story often retold, the martyr's love for the tramp. The hit man knows it well, believes in it, in love as redemption. He turns to the crucifix hammered to his wall, sets his eyes on the eyes of the Christ figure, and asks, "Got any other bright ideas?"

Matinee

I ought to be deliriously happy. The love of my life has called to invite me to the films. It's been ages since he last asked me to join him, to sit by his side to watch a movie, because I used to munch on popcorn, which got on his nerves. And because I pestered him, groping his groin, tickling his thigh, trying to get him to not waste the dark. It appears he is willing to give me another chance. "To see what?" I ask.

He tells me, "Two Norwegian films. *Hunger* and *Wolf at the Door.*" His affection is for depressing movies, the sort almost never produced in America, but often made in countries where it's winter most of the year. However, every once in a while, he flips and goes to a musical. His favorite is *Bye Bye Birdie*, which he considers an underrated gem.

Movies are his life and his livelihood, too. To keep bread on his table, a roof over his head, he spends most of his days in dark rooms watching movies. He is a voyeur. He'd rather watch other people live, die, have sex, than do it himself. Later, at night, by lamplight, he writes reviews, commentaries, criticisms of what he saw. Sometimes, he guest-lectures at film schools. He once told me that when he was younger, much younger, he entertained the notion of going to Hollywood, but didn't because he knew he'd hate the climate there. Also, he didn't think he was the movie-star type.

I disagreed. True, he is neither handsome nor very interesting to look at, "but," I told him, "you would've been great in *The Sorrow and the Pity.*"

I ask him if these Norwegian films are available on videotape. They are, but as I knew he would, he refuses my suggestion that we rent them, watch them not on hard seats but from the comfort of his bed. "You know how I feel about the small screen," he says. What he doesn't say, but what I know, is, he won't let me in his bed for any reason.

He came to see movies relatively late in life. The day he arrived in America was when he saw his first movie—a Western, a cowboy movie. He was already in his teens but didn't yet speak any English. I, having grown up with drive-ins and television, tried to imagine what that must have been like for him, but as with so many of his experiences, you really had to be there.

"It was rather terrifying," he told me. "I was escorted into a darkened theater and there, before my eyes, which were ignorant of the medium, horses stampeded, guns blazed, and more men in black hats came at me shouting things I didn't understand." I would've thought after such an experience he would have avoided the movies, but, apparently, he likes reliving the horror.

The love of my life needs to know if I'm going to meet him at the movies or not. "Should I wait for you?" he asks.

"No," I say. I have to say no because I have a date with the hit man, and there is no wriggling free of that. When I tell the love of my life, "I'm sorry, I'd like to go, really I would, but I can't," he doesn't ask why not. He doesn't accuse me of seeing someone else behind his back. He does not throw a fit nor make threats. He says only, "Okay, then. I'll call you another time."

I hold onto the receiver as if he were still there, still on the line with me, and I close my eyes as if I, too, could make my world disappear into the dark.

To Know the Extreme

*N*o sooner do I slip out of my coat and dress, does the hit man say, "I called you before, and the line was busy. Who were you talking to?"

"No one you know," I tell him. "An old friend." The hit man senses, although I am in his bed, I am not with him. My thoughts are elsewhere, and so he comes to sit very close. He puts a hand on my knee and says, "I've got this idea. We, you and me, should get walkie-talkies to hook us up for constant contact. We could always be in touch," he says. "Touch," he repeats, and his hand over my knee tightens. He is keen on hearing my voice when I ought to be inaccessible to him, while I'm bathing, or sitting in a secluded section of the park, or sleeping. He wants to listen to me sleep, eavesdrop on my dreams. He sugarcoats, in romantic words, what boils down to spying on me.

If we were hooked up with walkie-talkies, this is what would happen: I'd be in another bed when I'd hear the cackle of static. I'd ignore it, but it would persist. To muffle the plea to respond,

I'd stuff my walkie-talkie under the pillow. Later, the hit man would catch up to me and ask, "Why didn't you answer my call? Where were you? Tell me."

Walkie-talkies are out of the question. My face turns to stone, and I say, "You still don't trust me."

"We have to know the extremes," the hit man tells me. "The idea of trust doesn't exist without the lack of it." This is his philosophy, a strong belief of his people, their way of conducting business and love affairs. "But I trust you." His hand leaves my knee to stroke my cheek, my throat. "You tell me to trust you, and so I do."

My heart beats fast. No matter what he says, the fact is because of him, I'm jumpy, jittery, as if I'm being tailed.

Some nights he calls me on the phone just to ask what I had for dinner. Not wanting to get into it, to try and make him understand I'm not always hungry, I have lied and said, "A cheese sandwich, and a salad, and an orange."

In the moments that follow, when he echoes, "A cheese sandwich, a salad, an orange," I've experienced fear.

Because he hasn't yet figured out how to read what's on my mind, he detests the quiet. That I'm here with him but keeping things to myself unnerves him. He demands to know what I'm thinking about.

I could say, "Nothing. I'm just drifting," but he'd never let it go at that. So I tell him, "I was thinking about how you sort of resemble a schoolteacher I used to go out with."

Actually, there's no resemblance. The schoolteacher was lanky, sandy-haired, wore crewneck sweaters, drove a battered yellow Volkswagen, and considered himself my steady boyfriend.

I can't say what I considered him. Often, I thought of him as an intrusion. Late one afternoon, I was about to step into the shower when my bell rang. I was not expecting company. "Who's there?" I called into the intercom.

It was the schoolteacher dropping by uninvited. This was not the sort of surprise I greeted fondly, but grabbing a towel, wrapping it around myself sarong-style, I opened the door. "I'm about to take a shower," I said.

He sat on a chair, and I went to the bathroom. Letting the towel fall away, I turned on the tap and was ready to step under the spray of water when I remembered my robe draped over the couch.

I rewrapped myself in the towel and walked into this scene: The schoolteacher was squatting over my pile of dirty clothes. In his hands were my panties, spread to expose the crotch, which he was rubbing with his thumbs. So intent he was, he hadn't heard me, didn't sense my presence. Because I'd never seen anything quite like that, I watched for a while before asking, "What are you doing?"

He let out a wretched yap, not unlike the sound that heralded his orgasms. Also, he urinated a drop. A wet spot, the size of a silver dollar, appeared on his khakis. My panties fell from his hands.

An explanation was in order. This was the one he gave: When we're not together, I really miss you. And I get scared that maybe you're with someone else. With another man.

"Is that what you were doing? You were checking my panties for cum stains?"

He nodded, brighter, glad, as if I understood, as if it were now all perfectly okay. "I can't bear the thought of you making love with someone else," he said. "I just had to check, to be sure. I love you," he added, like that counted for something.

My skin crawled, invaded by skeeve. I felt violated in an extremely creepy way. "Get out," I told him. "Get out of here and never come back."

"I'm sorry," he begged. "It was only because I love you. I trust you. I do. I swear I do. I do trust you."

I held the door open for him.

Then I took my shower, and with a washcloth cleaned away another man's semen from between my legs.

That Little Exchange

*B*ecause he doesn't go for having his cock sucked, I suck on his thumb, blanket it in my tongue like a miniature frankfurter in a pastry puff. Not hard, I bite, just a nip, but the multimedia artist overreacts. "Ow," he pulls his finger from my mouth. "That hurt. I'm not a pervert, you know."

"Aw shucks," I say. "That's too bad."

Again, he reacts broadly. He laughs, and laughs, and laughs. Finally, he quits laughing and says, "I've got to write that one down." He gets up from the bed, puts pen to paper and asks, "You don't mind if I steal your words, do you?" As he's begun writing, I can't manage to tell him: Yes, I do mind.

"I'm doing a dialogue on panels," he explains. That little exchange is going to be painted red on red canvas and will be recorded so panels and voice will move something like singing in rounds.

I am not impressed with this crap he calls his art. I want to get back to the sex and ask, "So, where were we?"

He returns to my breasts and kneads them as if they were

dough for baking bread. Then he lets them go. "Oh, wait," he says. "Before I forget, do you know who's the new poetry editor at *The Kenyon Review?*"

On the table beside his bed are my cigarettes. If he's going to talk during sex, I might as well smoke during sex. "Is there something you want to tell me?" I blow out the match.

He inhales deeply, casts a glance downward and says, "My tool. It doesn't seem to be functioning properly."

Tool. His tool. I know the word is supposed to conjure up an image of things hard, things made of iron and steel—crowbars, hammers, man-sized screwdrivers—but when he says *tool*, I picture a Veg-O-Matic, a flimsy piece of tin you buy at Woolworth's, and it never works right either.

"I don't understand this," he says. "Does it happen much with your other men friends?" Aha! He has unwittingly divulged the source of his limp dick. He has assumed I make the same comparisons he makes, that I stack his dick up against other dicks. He is fearful his dick's vita pales alongside, that his dick's credentials aren't as spiffy as the next guy's. It's wilted under the scrutiny.

I could be gentle here and tell him all dicks droop now and again, but instead I say, "No. It's never happened with my other men friends." I don't want him getting any ideas that I could have anything to do with this, that I am the emasculating queen, the wicked witch of Limpland waving my craggy wand over once rigid cocks, turning them to jelly. "But," I make amends, "that doesn't mean anything. Each unto his own tool, right?"

And certainly to say, "You've seen one, you've seen them all," is erroneous. A spurious aphorism. While, yes, all cocks share certain characteristics, each one is unique, as are fingerprints, voices, handwritings, faces. They come big, small, thick, narrow, smooth, wrinkled, physically fit, able to perform on cue. Others

113

are gray in tint as if they chain-smoked Lucky Strikes and tire easily. I once knew one with a crook, like it was double-jointed.

Men recognize, grant independence, consider their cocks little friends, secret buddies. They name them: Melvin, Wilbur, PJ, Pooky.

I've heard of women bestowing cute twin names on their breasts: Meg & Peg, June & Jane, Winky & Blinky. Probably the same women who collect dolls from around the world in native costume. But never have I heard of a woman saying, "How about going down on old Vivian," or "Stick it to Florence," the way men ask you to give Herman a kiss or show Jimbob a good time.

There's a saying that goes: It's not the size of the shoes, but the rhythm of the feet.

Or something like that.

Often, men with big ones think that's the whole story, whip them out, put them on display, expect me to gasp and go silly with gratitude.

Size really doesn't matter, just as long as there's *some* bulk, *some* dimension to it. You do have to know it's there.

The littlest cock I ever knew might not have been the smallest one in recorded history, but I never saw one that size on a postpubescent male. It was no bigger than my index finger, all the way around. I could tell he'd entered me only by studying his face. When his expression turned beatific, I groaned.

Experience with the littlest cock taught me something. A less-than-ideal situation can be salvaged. I tell the multimedia artist, "More than one path can bring us to the same destination." I smile, sagelike, as if there were wisdom to my words, as if I were quoting Confucius: When cock go limp like noodle, eat hearty lunch.

I expect an artist to dote on breasts. Preoccupation with shape,

form. The multimedia artist's art, however, is cerebral, con-
trived, hasn't a thing to do with bosoms. This is reflected in the
way he's at mine. He lacks finesse. He makes noises—blub,
blub, blub—like blowing bubbles into milk through a straw. His
frenzy is peculiar, and I'm thinking he might drool on me when
he whimpers, bleats, "Mommy."

I push him away, get up from his bed and say, "I've got to
write that one down."

Seven Tales of Famine

I pull up a fourth chair, marring the continuity of the Kessel sisters. They are huddled together as if in a conspiracy. "What's going on?" I ask.

"Boy trouble," the middle one says, very sympathetically. I am to understand it is not her boy trouble.

"I got dumped," the youngest volunteers.

"Oh," I pick up the menu, scan it for meatless dishes, and the youngest sister whines at me, "I don't expect you to understand, but you could at least pretend to feel sorry for me."

"But I don't feel sorry for you," I say. "I'm sorry you got dumped, but, hey, it happens."

"Not to you it doesn't."

"Of course it does."

"When?" the middle sister challenges. "Tell us."

"Yeah. Who dumped you?" The eldest sister has joined forces with the middle one.

I) My heart went thump, thump. I'd been singled out by the

biggest deal my high school had to offer. Me. A lowly freshman. In a few months he'd go off to college, to Brown, but that night, at a party that spilled from the house to the lawn, he led me behind a row of bushes. He had a reputation for being fast.

The ground was cool against my legs. A fleeting kiss, and bypassing second base, he slid a hand up my thigh. I was a virgin then. Not that I was saving myself for anything special. I had no notions of the event as pictured in a Laura Ashley ad — muted, lace gown, honeysuckle in a vase by the bed, an image to save like a photograph in a silver frame. Still, a quickie behind some bushes didn't suit me. Also, I wasn't sure if he knew my name. I'd have wanted him to know my name, so I clamped my hand to his wrist and said, "I don't want to do something I'll regret." That was a gamble because I did want to be with him, to smooch, let him feel under my bra.

"I admire you," he said. "How you know yourself. That's commendable." Then he said, "Wait here. I'll be right back."

I sat up, lotus position, which I thought implied I was deep, did yoga, meditated. And I waited. Waited until my legs cramped, until the party broke up, dissolved. So I didn't do anything I might've regretted. Yet I experienced regret nonetheless.

II) A stupid, clumsy gesture. Showing me her picture. Blond, leggy, wearing a modest tank suit, she was stepping from the surf at Hilton Head. "I'm in love with her," he said. She was an Episcopalian, right-handed.

Next he told me this: Over the weekend her parents came to New York. Very much she wanted him to meet Mummy and Daddy. But there was a small hitch. Mummy and Daddy would be deeply distressed to learn their precious was being porked by a New York Catholic boy. That he was in medical school wouldn't carry any weight with them. So she hit upon a plan.

She introduced him as a friend of a friend who would show them around New York as only an ethnic could. "Won't that be fun?" she said.

"And you agreed to this?" I was appalled.

"I had no choice. I'm in love with her."

Letting him believe I cared that I'd lost him, I forced out two teardrops. Generous of me, a kindness committed because he'd have plenty of other indignities ahead of him.

III) I spun, did cartwheels for a man old enough to be my father and then some. He was not handsome or dashing, but irresistible. He was thin, his bones were knobby, as if he never got the hang of eating well. There was ash on his hands.

He treated my declarations of love as bits of girlish silliness. Cute, charming, a delight, but meaningless. "Come, come," he said. "If I took up with you, you'd go running off in two weeks flat. And where would that leave me? A lonely old man abandoned by his young, beautiful, coldhearted lover."

"I'd never leave you. Never," I insisted. "I love you, and you don't believe me. It's tragic."

"Oh yes," he mocked me, teasing. "Very tragic indeed."

IV) It could've been the times. It seemed everyone went rushing backwards—blindfolds on, trousers zipped—to old-fashioned values. Even the musician—a member of a group generally renowned for having the morals of snakes—was suddenly disturbed at sex with a married woman. "It's not right," he said, "the way you're with me for an hour or two and then go home to your husband. God," he said, "you've been married only, what? Six months. What'd you get married for anyway?"

"To try to secure a lover," I said, and he, mistakenly, thought I meant him. "Where did you get the idea I'd rather you were married?" he asked. "I'm sorry," he said, "but I can't see you anymore."

No one had explicitly dumped me since I was nineteen and thrown over for a debutante, which I couldn't manage to feel bad about. Consequently, I wasn't familiar with the protocol. What does one do when one is dumped? Cry? Beg? Surely I was expected to do something. So I did this: I spat in his face. Very childish—not to mention disgusting—but I was glad I did it.

V) My father went off to his office, where he went two days a week. The other days, he worked at the hospital. Midmorning, my mother was baking cookies while I looked on, hoping I'd get to lick the bowl, when Nurse called wanting to know where the hell was the doctor, she had a waiting room jammed with blood-diseased patients. The bowl of cookie dough fell to the floor and broke. My mother called the police, and I picked out the chocolate chips and ate them.

VI) I went out for a walk, and by coincidence came upon my friend, the boy, walking his dog. I apologized for not returning his last phone call. "I've been busy," I said.

The boy was only a few years younger than me, but they were significant years. He held me in great esteem.

Nothing physical had ever happened between us, although as of late, we'd been pussyfooting in that direction. It might've been, then, the hour of the night, the glow of the moon acting as a catalyst. The dog was the first to catch on, jumping excitedly, sniffing crotches.

The boy lived on Avenue B. His apartment was a rat hole. That's how young he was. Still holding the notion that scuzzy places were romantic, he confused the trappings of poverty with sensitivity. I was not enchanted by the mattress on the floor nor by the cockroaches scurrying into cracks in the linoleum.

I closed my eyes to the grime, and we kissed. He broke away first, hung his head and said, "I can't go through with this. Our friendship is valuable to me. I'm afraid of ruining it."

I heard him, what he said, the words he used, but this is what registered: He said no.

He was younger than me, but, perhaps, smarter. Alas, I wasn't in the mood for wisdoms. Annoyed, and even a bit crushed, I said, "That's the difference between us. To me, your friendship's not all that valuable. I'd have risked it."

VII) The love of my life has to count for more than one loss. "What can I do?" I rubbed my leg against his under the small wooden table at a café on Bleecker Street. "It's been seven years. Seven years of my life devoted to you."

He raised an eyebrow, skeptical, and I conceded, "So it hasn't been exclusive devotion, but I had to do something to try and get my mind off you. Seven years, and frankly, I'm running out of tricks. Give me a hint," I asked. "How can I make you happy?"

"You do make me happy," he said, but he looked so unhappy, I scrounged for another effort. "How's this?" I offered. "Suppose I bake treats for you? Pies. I'll bake pies for you. Cherry. Rhubarb. Peach."

He leaned back in his chair and laughed. Worth noting because it was something he so rarely did. "That's the sweetest thing anyone has ever said to me. So sweet, I almost believe you would bake me pies."

"I would," I insisted. "You must believe me."

"I don't deserve you." His laughter, any trace of it, was gone. "I've done nothing to deserve you."

He was wrong. He'd done everything to deserve me. I was the one indebted to him, for I'd not suffered any trials, triumphed over nothing, not plague, not locusts, not famine.

The Kessel sisters are quiet. Communicating telepathically, no doubt. Then the youngest speaks. "So, in other words," she says, "you have no idea how I'm feeling."

"No," I agree. "I guess not."

Going for Distance

*A*s compensation, I suspect, for his tool not functioning when we were last together, the multimedia artist is going for distance. It's up, and damn it, it's going to stay up. Steady he moves, as if sex were a marathon, pacing himself as if he had many miles more to go. To accomplish this feat, he controls his breathing. He does not moan, groan, sigh, whimper, but the real trick is to think of something else, to imagine I'm not here, that he's not on top of, inside of me, that sex isn't sex, but chiseling marble or tracking baseball statistics.

Keeping a dick hard for the long haul isn't worth the effort. Boredom sets in, leaving me little to do other than, in turn, think of other things, too.

I think of the time I had a darling boyfriend, the college soccer team goalie. An adorable couple, we were mismatched, ill-suited to one another. Between classes, we smooched on College Walk. In the evenings, we went out for pizza and beer. I helped him with his homework.

I don't know how many young athletes feel this way about

their coaches, but my goalie rated his coach top banana. The coolest, the smoothest dreamboat of a father figure. "You know what Coach did?" he'd say. "You know what Coach said?" The coach's exploits consisted of incidents like this one: The coach pulled his car into a gas station. The attendant came over and asked, "Fill it up?" and the coach said, "No, empty it out."

My goalie thought that was a scream, a stitch, a howl and a half. Also, my goalie admired the coach's personal life, his wife, his two angelic daughters. My goalie wanted to become a man exactly like his coach.

The coach's wife was pretty, but fading fast. On her way to looking tired, cheap, as if she were hitting the hooch. Those cheerleader looks hold for only so long before washing out. I never exchanged more than two words with the woman, but I heard from my goalie, who'd heard it repeatedly from his coach, she was no deep thinker. So, if my goalie wanted to become a man exactly like his coach, dating me was not the way to get there. I was never going to be a dim ex-cheerleader with a husband who made snide comments about my intellect to a bunch of snot-nosed jocks.

On nights before soccer games, the coach sent his team to bed early, to ensure they were well rested, didn't sap their strength, to maintain peak performance level.

Back then, the legal drinking age was eighteen. Every college had a pub, and after some hours at the library, I moseyed over to ours.

It was too busy, too noisy, too much effort to make out any one face in the Friday night crowd. I stuck around, intending to have one beer before going back to my room.

I sipped from my bottle of Rolling Rock when someone behind me asked, "So where's the goalie?" It was the coach.

"Sleeping," I said. "Aren't you the one who decrees they're in bed by nine?" That they were to be in bed alone was axiomatic.

"Yeah," he said, "but I didn't think anyone actually listened to me." With a nod of his head, he pointed out a rowdy, rambunctious group gathered at one table. The soccer team was tanked, whooping it up. One of the Argentine ones wore a bra around his head so the cups fit like earmuffs. The goalie, I gathered, was the only member of the soccer team to take the coach's instructions literally and to heart.

Preventing a tightly knit line of girls from cutting between us as, like ducklings, they made their way to the bar, the coach stepped in close to me. Very close. "You know," he said, "it's probably none of my business, but what is it you see in him, the goalie? After all, he's a good kid. A very good kid."

"And I'm not?" I asked.

"I didn't say that. I meant, well, he is just a kid."

That was, of course, precisely what I saw in him. As if I could see my own future, I knew my goalie was a final fling, the last sweet young boy I'd know, the last boy who'd hold my hand and carry my schoolbooks, a boy who went to bed when his coach told him to.

"You're too much for him," the coach said. "He doesn't know what to do with you."

I shrugged. It was an open shrug, as if to say I were ready for another suggestion.

We went to my room. I kicked off my boating shoes, slipped out of my chinos. The coach unbuttoned my Oxford shirt. Stepping back, he studied me as if I were a statue. "Your body is magnificent," he said. "Don't ever wear baggy college clothes again." This was nothing like telling me to be in bed by nine before a game. It was another kind of command.

Oh yeah, the coach was cool. Very cool. So cool that while fucking, he kept me guessing. He never gave up a sound. Because I was going on about oooh, how good it was, all the usual claptrap, I started to feel foolish. So I went quiet, too. To keep quiet, I thought about something else. I thought about the goalie, how in bed he was like an enthusiastic puppy. So much so, I once worried he'd piddle on my sheets.

The quiet grew unnerving. I quit moving and asked the coach, "Hey, are you with me here?"

"Sure, I'm with you." Then he whispered, "You've met your match, baby."

There it went, without much fanfare, the remains of innocence gone, broken as easily as a promise.

To the soccer game I wore a snug skirt, a slinky blouse, high-heeled pumps. I sat in the stands two rows behind the coach. Our team was winning hands down. It was a game hardly worth watching. Nothing could get by my goalie. At halftime, the score was a remarkable three to zip.

At the start of the third quarter, the coach leaned over to his assistant, said something, and stood up. He turned, and climbed over the bleachers. As he passed, he signaled for me to follow.

His office in the gymnasium was a short walk from the field and was equipped with a couch. He shimmied my skirt up over my hips.

We got back to the game moments before it ended, and although we did win, it wasn't a shutout. The final score was four to two. Two shots whizzed past the goalie as he was searching the stands for his coach and for his girlfriend.

Another Hunger

*T*he multimedia artist rolls off of me and says, "Wow. That was great."

"Huh?" My mind is still elsewhere. "Oh, yeah, great." I smile weakly.

"Couldn't have done it without you." He kisses the tip of my nose, and he gets up, walks to his kitchen. There, he gets an orange. One orange. He brings it into the bed, peels it, pushes his thumbs into the center. Juice squirts as the orange breaks apart. I expect him to offer me half, or at least a piece, but he doesn't.

He pops the last slice into his mouth, chomps with gusto, and I say, "I'm hungry."

"You are?"

"Yes." The aerobic workout he meant to pass off as sex gave me an appetite. "I didn't have any orange. I need food."

On the subject of blow-jobs, the hit man once said: There are two kinds of girls.

On the subject of food: There are two kinds of men. Those

who would feed you, until, like a dog, you'd eat yourself to death. And then there are those who feed themselves while you happen to be there.

"I can order up some Chinese food, if you want." The multimedia artist makes it sound as if this required effort, as if he were doing me a big favor.

"That's fine," I say, and as he goes to the telephone, I call out to remind him, "Nothing with meat for me. And not that bean curd either. I can't stomach bean curd."

The hit man prepares me lavish meals, from scratch: gnocchi, eggplant, thick-crusted breads, desserts of sesame cookies, anisette toast. Even when it's not mealtime, he presses food on me: grapes, cherries, melon balls, a pear he slices into bite-sized chunks. We eat and fuck and eat and fuck and fuck and eat. What would bring it all home for him is to have sex in the kitchen, fuck on the countertop, on a bed of tomatoes and artichoke hearts, a loaf of bread for a pillow. The hit man keeps me full, sated, gratified beyond capacity.

I used to deprive myself of food because, somehow, I'd gotten the idea women weren't supposed to have big appetites. Women were expected to pick, peck, nibble. It was then my habit to, before a date, stuff myself, devour, inhale a bag of potato chips. That way, after a feminine two mouthfuls of dinner, I'd be able to put down my fork and truthfully say, "I'm full," the picture of the dainty morsel I purported to be kept intact.

I did not connect appetite with appetite. The stupidity of this assessment was revealed to me on a hot summer night when I went to Sedutto's, and because I was alone, got a double cone. Two scoops of cherry vanilla. Cone in hand, I walked along licking, scooping ice cream with my tongue. And I noticed men were staring at me with desire on their lips. To judge from their expressions, and also from that one man who said, "Oh, to be an ice cream cone," I was doing more than eating ice cream, licking more than cherry vanilla.

Our Chinese food arrives. The multimedia artist puts the brown paper bag on the table, and he studies the bill. "Let's see," he says, "yours comes to $7.35."

He wants money in hand before setting out the food, as if he could send it back should I not pay up. Without comment, I go to my bag, get a $10 bill.

"I don't have change," he tells me.

"Keep it," I say, and he does.

Dutch treat irks me. Two people engaging in sex ought to afford each other additional generosities.

He portions the food onto the complimentary paper plates and lays out the chopsticks. He gives nothing, and he keeps the condiments—the mustard, the duck sauce—and the tea bags off to the side. Later, he will stash them in his cabinet.

We eat, and he steals sidelong glances at my food. "They make great string beans in black bean sauce, don't they?" he says.

"Yes," I concur. "Very good."

"I usually get that for myself."

"Then why didn't you?" I ask, and he tells me it seemed excessive to get two orders of the same thing. "We could share," he says.

He got, for himself, shredded beef and cabbage. "I can't eat that," I tell him what he already knows. This is what he means by *share*: He will gobble up half of my food without having to give me any of his.

Eye of the Needle

*B*efore I even have a chance to knock, the hit man opens his door. He's been waiting, poised, listening for my footsteps in the hall.

He yanks me inside his apartment, and he pounces. His arms circle me, his mouth covers mine. He eats away my lipstick, kisses my teeth, tongue, tonsils. With his foot, he kicks the door closed, neglects to lock it.

Like the Hindu deity Shiva, the hit man seems to have more than one pair of hands. Hands are everywhere at once. Caressing my arms, my back, grabbing my ass, my thighs, pushing my legs apart, fondling my breasts, lifting my dress, tugging at my panties, unzipping his fly. A frenzy of activity.

I step out of my underwear, and he is out of his clothes, on his bed, cock waving high.

I sit over him, and my dress—full-skirted, teal blue—billows out over us, like a parachute, covering, concealing the act. Yet we expose plenty. Fucking with my clothes on is very titillating, smutty. I go for this.

A drop of sweat winds down my face and falls into his open mouth. He swallows sweat, musk, and his tongue darts across his lips, a thirsty man, parched. He wants more, more to fill his mouth. In pursuit, he sticks a hand down the front of my dress. I hear the rip, feel the fabric tear away. But so what? If the room around us were to catch fire, flames licking the walls, we would go out in the blaze. We are intent only on our pleasure.

The hit man shudders, moans, calls to his Jesus. Soon after, I melt, ooze warm, smile.

But still, the hit man is disappointed, has a regret. He wishes we came together, shared one orgasm between us, as if it were a chocolate malt with two straws. "That never happens for us. You know, two hearts beating as one."

I grimace. "Simultaneous orgasms are coincidence, that's all," I say. What I don't say is: What's mine is mine, ought to be distinctly mine without confusion.

Lying back and smoking a cigarette, I feel the wet slither out, spread, and I get up to clean myself off.

"Uh-oh," the hit man points out needlessly, "the back of your dress. It's stained. You got the makings of a small Italian village there."

"I know. It'll wash off. But this," I touch where my dress is torn, where the seam was ripped apart. "This could be a problem. I can't go home like this. It looks like I was raped."

"Ravished," he corrects me.

It isn't likely he would have a safety pin, an item so cautious, but I ask anyway.

"I doubt it," he says. "But I do have a needle and thread." He goes to his dresser, opens a drawer, and I confess, "I don't know how to sew."

He shakes his head at the wonderment that is me. "Then it's a good thing I know how."

Moving to sit under the floor lamp, he bends under the light. His face is, in part, illuminated, and I watch him lick the end of the thread, steady it through the eye of the needle. Deftly, he makes a knot.

I start to take the dress off, holding the hem to pull it up over my head, to give it to him to fix, but he says no. He beckons me to come near, to stand close to him.

Under the light, he takes the fabric of my dress, joins the seams and sews neat, sweet stitches as if it were me he were mending.

Three

An Out-of-Body Experience

*D*uring the act of intercourse, I am, should I choose, able to perform this trick: Slip away, have an out-of-body experience, take no part in the activity other than to hover above watching two people rut. Sometimes even that was too much to stomach, and I'd leave the room entirely, float off to a movie or the beach. I did, however, return for the orgasm. It shouldn't be a total loss.

When this happened, when I disengaged from my lower body parts, when my attention took leave, I took it as a message from God: Don't bother having sex with this guy again.

The upshot is: I've been intimate with men whom I haven't been remotely intimate with. Technically, we fucked, but I can't say I was there for it.

What I can't distance myself from is kissing. Kissing requires my presence, my participation. The mouth is too near the eyes, the brain, the throat, for me to disassociate. Kissing is up-close, personal, and decidedly involves two.

While pretty much everyone kisses, those who kiss well are

like butterflies. With the assurance of natural instinct, a good kiss flutters, glides, soars, swoops, and perches on some unnamed spot causing me to swoon, to think: I could go on kissing like this forever.

It was a summer evening, late July or early August, when the love of my life and I went walking. I was giddy to be with him away from the confines of café tables or the arms of movie theater seats keeping us apart. How I got him to agree to an evening stroll escapes me. Perhaps it just happened. I wore a white eyelet dress, white cotton panties, sandals, that was all. The night was hot and muggy. No stars twinkled in the sky. We walked along the river, past the hustlers, the whores, the junkies, the homeless sleeping on cardboard beds. Past the bleakness, we sidestepped into an alleyway. Cobblestoned, narrow, crooked, tilting, sinking with time, the buildings on both sides looked as if they once were stables.

There, I kissed him. He kissed me, too. Oh, such kisses! Dear kisses, each one a couplet. It seemed impossible to stop, to let go of such kisses, but I managed to pull away, to ruin everything. "Let's go to my place," I said.

Later, and throughout the years after, I've gone looking for that cobblestoned alley, as if finding it would recapture what was lost. All along the river I have walked, poked, nosed around corners. I have asked people, "Do you know of an alleyway off the river? Cobblestoned? Maybe lit by gas lamps?" But no one knew of such a place, and I began to think, not that I'd imagined it, but that the love of my life and I had been transported to another place, another time, on the wings of a kiss. We could stay there only as long as the kiss lasted. Something magical happened that night. An out-of-body experience, although nothing like the one when I leave the bed where I'm having sex.

Earlier today, late in the morning, the hit man called me up and said, "Meet me. I need to get out. I've got to ventilate. Meet me, and we'll take a walk."

It's not summer. It's early winter, cold enough to make frost with my breath. I wear a sweater, a coat, a hat. I join up with the hit man at the corner of Hudson and Bank Streets. "Let's go to the river," he takes me by the sleeve. He wears black leather gloves, leaves no fingerprints.

We sit on the pier. Hoboken is on the other side, across the water. We smoke cigarettes, and when we're done with them, I say, "It's freezing out here. Come on, let's go."

Two blocks south he steers me across the street. I take another step and stop, locked in time. "This is it," I say. "It's here."

"Charles Lane," the hit man tells me. "This is Charles Lane. You've never come this way before?"

"Once," I whisper. "Once before."

"It's wonderful, isn't it? One of the few remaining old, old streets. An original. There are a couple of others like it but further downtown." The hit man is talking to the wind. I'm not listening because it's summer again. I have on my white eyelet dress, and it's not clear to me if I am heartbroken or not.

The hit man reaches out and draws me to him. And we kiss. A kiss that becomes a kiss from the past, before evolving to another kiss. But not any other kiss. This kiss, too, is of another world. I feel as if I am levitating, as if my feet are inches off the cobblestones. And I think: I could go on kissing like this forever.

"Hey," the hit man breaks away, "what do you say we go to my place?"

A Parable

I reach for a cigarette, sit at the edge of the bed, ashtray resting on my thigh, my feet now firmly on the floor.

The hit man gets up to put on aqua blue jockeys, black T-shirt, and he says, "You're it. The one I was meant to be with. Like it or not, there's no one else for me. I know this. You're my mate for life."

I want to tell him a story. A love story I learned of from a public television documentary. I say, "Listen up," and I relate what I think is an important story, crucial: On one of the Galápogos Islands, until recently, there lived a flourishing population of sea turtles. Large sea turtles, the sort featured in deep-sea mythologies. Alas, like the brontosaurus, the woolly mammoth, the dodo bird, these turtles vanished. Gone—poof—no more. Just like that, without a word of explanation, the lot of them were wiped out. Except for one. Oddly, one turtle survived the devastation that destroyed the others of its kind.

There are two facts to know about this species of turtle: 1) their life expectancy, barring whatever it was that killed them all but one, is one hundred and fifty years—a long time—and 2)

138

these turtles are monogamous—mate for life—their marriages endure for over a century.

Also, there are two things to know about our turtle, the surviving turtle: 1) it's male and 2) he's estimated to be just shy of thirty years old. In the sea-turtle span, a babe.

He's got a long way to go, to eat bugs, snooze on a rock in the sun, swim, frolic in the water, lead the good life. Except for one hitch: He doesn't have a mate, will never have a mate. Like Leviathan, the Loch Ness Monster, Sasquatch, this turtle has had celibacy, loneliness, thrust upon him.

It occurs to me, but I leave this out of the story, that the love of my life is also like that turtle. All his people are gone, too.

The turtle, unfortunately, is unable to grasp such a twist of fate, make sense of it, so each day our turtle journeys up onto a rocky cliff, cranes his sinewy turtle neck, and calls for her. He cries in pursuit of his lady turtle. He keens, wails a love song, his mating call, into an abyss. For at least a hundred years more, he will do this, each and every day. There are a lot of days in a hundred plus years, but he'll never catch on: She isn't coming. She doesn't exist.

"Can't he mate with another kind of sea turtle?" the hit man asks a reasonable question. I give him the answer the naturalist narrating the program gave. "No. No other turtle will respond to his particular call. Nature is very careful that way."

Overwhelmed by such a hideous plight, the hit man is speechless, almost crushed, nearly destroyed, but he finds something, a possibility, and he brightens. "Hey," he says, "you know, the ocean is pretty fucking big. I'll bet there's another one out there, his female, swimming around. She'll find him eventually. Don't you think that? I mean, come on, the ocean, the fucking ocean, it goes on forever."

The hit man shoots for the happy ending, the ending where it all works out justly, but it's an ending that isn't going to happen, not ever, not in one hundred plus years.

Mirror, Mirror

As if we've been married for twelve, thirteen, thirty-seven years to each other, the multimedia artist and I, on the heels of a ho-hum roll in the hay, are in bed reading. I might as well smear cold cream on my face, stick a few curlers in my hair.

He's reading *The Journal of Deliberately Obscure Babble*, a title and subtitle cluttered with *neos, isms, dialectics*. It's a string of words I can't grip.

I scan one of those freebie newspapers left for the taking in grocery stores, copy shops, laundromats, when the multimedia artist looks up and tells me a joke.

Question: Why do Jewish women make love with their eyes closed?

Answer: They can't bear watching someone else have a good time.

I don't laugh, don't toss off so much as a polite smile to indicate I, at least, got it.

Perhaps he thinks, simply, his joke wasn't a good joke, wasn't funny. Or maybe because he's not a regular teller of jokes, his rhythm is off. "Wait, wait," he gropes his memory. "I've got another one. What do Jewish women make for dinner?"

"Reservations," I answer tersely.

"You've heard that one before?"

"I've heard them all before."

He goes back to his reading, and I turn the pages of the newspaper with a crackle. A loud, exasperated sigh worms out from me, groans at the surface.

"Did you say something?" the multimedia artist asks.

"No, I didn't *say* anything."

He doesn't pursue the source of the noise, leaving me no choice but to repeat it.

"Is something the matter?"

"Yes," I say. "The tedium here is getting to me."

"Tedium? What tedium?"

"This. You. Reading in bed after sex, sex that bordered on necrophilia, except you're not quite dead. No, you're just waiting to die. For someone who fancies himself the innovative hipster, you are one dull potato."

"An innovative hipster? I never referred to myself as an innovative hipster."

"You don't have to say it," I point out. "You exude it. So fab, so hip, two baby steps ahead of the mainstream, setting trends the world over. Well, I'm not fooled. You haven't come up with a truly original thought yet." When I quit talking, I'm surprised to discover his expression reveals pain, a wound like internal bleeding. "What's wrong?" I ask. "Are you sick?"

"I'm hurt," he says. "You, your words, hurt me."

"Really? Seriously?"

"Yes, really. Don't you think I have feelings?"

I answer him truthfully. "No. Or at least not such sensitive ones." Then, in defense of myself, I say, "Yeah, well, you hurt my feelings with those Jewish women jokes."

"No, I didn't," he says. "Those jokes weren't about you. You don't even look Jewish." He marks his place in the journal with a paper clip, and he brings his face close to mine. I assume he's zooming in for a kiss. I moisten my lips, and he says, "We are not of like minds."

"Huh?"

"It appears you believe that we, you and I, are very similar in disposition, that we hold similar values, morals, hopes, ideas. But, in fact, we are of very different temperaments."

"You think I don't know that?" We have little in common. He is false, pretentious. I am up-front, honest. Or at least honest enough to admit perhaps he's not completely wrong. I do assume we share some traits. Such as: when you get down to it, we don't give a fuck about one another.

"For instance," he says. "I can't be as cavalier about this as you are. This," he waves his hand over the bed with me in it, "is difficult for me. There are conflicts. I suffer from the turmoil. But for you, it's merely fun and games."

Very easily I could quip: It's not all that much fun. But I keep my mouth shut lest I win his argument for him.

"To me," he goes on, "to me ... well, I feel deeply. I care a great deal about things, ideas, people."

Things, ideas, people, and in that order, is as far as he dares to take this caring of his. Things. Ideas. People. In the abstract. Nothing, no one, in particular. Oh, it turns out he and I are plenty alike after all. Only he's not as far along, as well developed, as me. A lump of coal to a glass-cutting diamond. I am the reflection of what he might become, although he's got a long way to go.

Why Is a Good Question

The Kessel sisters sit in judgment. A triumvirate determining the outcome of my affair with the multimedia artist—what will be.

"He must have some good qualities." The youngest sister is kindest of heart. "What is it you like about him?"

"We have the same coloring. We could be of the same people."

The Kessel sisters appreciate the joy of sameness, but it's not enough. The middle sister, the pragmatist, asks, "What does he do for you? What's in it for you to stay with him?"

"He takes me to gallery openings where, often, the hors d'oeuvres are delicious. And the people there are interesting to watch, like an alien culture. And," I add, "I have lovely orgasms with him." A phenomenon defying explanation. There's no accounting for such orgasms. Sex with him—the ins and outs of it—is drab, rote. An active fantasy is a necessity to aid and abet the process along. Yet I experience dreamy orgasms. Go figure it. Orgasms that begin in my belly before spreading out

143

like an oil slick, moving warm, thick, gooey to my fingertips and toes.

"Let's get to the down side." The eldest Kessel sister keeps track of his faults.

"Selfish. Stingy, cheap. Pedestrian of mind but elitist in attitude. Self-centered, and aside from the dreamy orgasms, he's a lousy lay."

"Be specific." The eldest sister is after details, examples, illustrations.

I offer her some choice ones: He eats food in front of me without giving me any. He has never treated me to anything, not even a cup of coffee. After we fuck, he gets up and makes phone calls. The only compliment he's ever given me is to tell me I don't look Jewish, and he's got some kind of grudge against oral sex.

Still, the Kessel sisters feel there is not sufficient evidence to tip the scales of justice either way. "You're holding out on us," the middle one says. "What have you left out?"

"Nothing. Except, just this." I tell them: Done, we broke apart. My eyes closed, my body limp, I heard his voice, seemingly distant, although I knew perfectly well he was right next to me. "Do you like basketball?" he asked.

"No," I said.

"Oh. The St. John's game is on. They're playing Villanova. One of the great games of the season."

As if I didn't know the answer, I asked, "Do you want to watch it?"

"Yeah, I do."

"So, watch. Don't mind me."

And he didn't mind me. I lit a cigarette, flipped through *Artforum*, looked at the pictures, while he was at the television fiddling with the antenna. Satisfied with the reception, he hopped onto the bed.

The way you skip a rock across a lake, I skimmed *Artforum* across the room and asked myself: What am I doing here?

In the folds of the sheet, I found my panties. "I'm going to go now," I said.

"Already? So soon? Go! Go! Go, damn it! Go!" he shouted, and I asked, "Do you mind if I dress first?"

He laughed, "Not you. I didn't mean you. Number sixteen had the ball and was standing there with it like a dufus. Holding."

"I'm missing a stocking," I told him. "Have you seen it?"

"Yes!" His fist shot into the air.

"So where it is?"

"I don't know. But it couldn't have just walked off. You'll find it." How cold to be indifferent at the loss of the very stocking he caressed not an hour before.

I found it—the lost stocking—coiled around a chair leg the way a garden hose knots itself. After freshening my lipstick, I gathered up my coat and my bag, and said, "See you."

"If you can wait until halftime," he said, "I'll walk you out."

"No. I can't wait until halftime."

His head—riveted as if his neck were broken, set, pinned with steel bolts—was rigid, but his eyes, fixed on the basketball, danced, darted, glided as the ball was dribbled, tossed, shot, and missed. "No! When can I see you again?"

"Are you talking to me?" I asked.

"Of course I'm talking to you. When can I see you again?"

I wanted to know why. "Why do you want to see me again?"

"Why?" he echoed. "What kind of question is that?"

"*Why* is a good question," I said.

"Because I had a great time with you tonight. I always have a great time with you. I like you," he said. Still more attentive to the basketball game than to me, he added, "I like you a lot."

It wasn't exactly the same thing as a dreamy orgasm, but

a warmth did spread through me, leaving me weak, gelatinous, not quite able to stand on my own, and I said, "Oh. Okay. Call me."

The Kessel sisters, sitting on their couch in a row, cry out in unison, "Dump him!" as if they were the Del Rubio Triplets. "Dump him," they sing.

Part of My Other Life

What do you think of Jules?" The hit man sits at the edge of his bed, stroking my legs, calves and ankles.

"Jewels?" I picture baubles, gems, ropes of pearls spilling from a treasure chest.

"Jules," he repeats. "I want us to name our first son Jules. And get this, our second child, a girl, we'll call Tosca. Tosca," he gives the word a romantic spin. "Isn't that beautiful? Tosca. From the opera, you know. So, what do you think? Jules and Tosca."

"Jules and Tosca. It sounds like a foreign film. Subtitled. On the screen it would read *Jules et Tosca*."

"No, come on, really. What do you think?" He can't be asking what do I think, really. Naming fictional babies has to be play, like foreplay, only after.

"Tosca's okay. But Jules ... I don't know about Jules. It lends itself to ridicule. Family Jules and all that. Besides, aren't you supposed to name babies after saints?"

"Yeah, but ... " he makes a face, "fuck that."

"I'm supposed to name them for the dead," I tell him.

147

"Oh, that explains it." The hit man has always wondered why no Jewish guys were called Junior or Sonny or Little Irving. "You know," he says, "as opposed to Big Irv, the father." Continuing with this nonsense, the hit man next asks where we'll live. "With two kids," he says, "we'll need a house."

Is there danger in pretending we'll have babies, naming them as if they were cats? Is there harm in talking about where we'll never live? Can make-believe lead to trouble?

"I think we ought to get a modest house on Long Island," the hit man says.

"Why do Brooklynites aspire to modest houses on Long Island?" I ask. "Where do you people get the idea Dix Hills is a step up?"

The hit man looks baffled. Perhaps Long Island is a dream he's not ready to surrender. Also, he's thinking of something else. "You realize," he says, "when you're pregnant, this will be different," he gestures at the bed. "Once you're well along, we won't be able to carry on like we do now."

That's it! That does it! Puts the kibosh on further flights of fancy. Only he's unaware I've folded, quit, and he asks, "How do you feel about Jersey?"

I sit up in his narrow bed, turn away from the crucifix, the holy picture. I face him and his earnestness. "If we got married and had two kids," I say, "we'd be living in hell."

"Don't laugh," he cups my chin with his fingers, holds me steady. "You laugh, and I'm serious. I want us to make a life together."

"We have a life together," I tell him. "This, what we have, is our life together."

"It's not enough. I want to come home to you. I'm very serious about that. And I'm calm now."

I try not to think about what he's saying. If I think too much about it, I get a chill.

148

"I want us to live together," he says again. "The rest, the particulars, kids, houses, that's not important. That we can work
out later. What's important is us. Together."

I try to imagine living with the hit man. Our life together.
This is what I come up with: We'd live in the Bronx. Not Brooklyn, because Brooklyn is his and would engulf me, swallow me
whole. So we'd live in the Bronx. On the Grand Concourse, the
tree-lined avenue as wide as a boulevard, where the prewar apart-
ments are spacious, with high ceilings, and hallways that retain
odors of foods cooked fifty, sixty years before.

Our apartment would be splendorous and shabby. The moldings would be baroque, but chipped, paint peeling away. Rooms
would be divided by French doors, crystal knobs, glass cracked.
Our bathroom floor would be marble, pink. The tub would have
legs. We'd trade his narrow bed for a bigger one, but not much
bigger because we'd sleep entwined beneath the crucifix.

I'd do the grocery shopping. Each day, I'd go out only to buy
food. Not at a supermarket. I'd shop lovingly at the greengrocer,
the bakery, the cheese store. I'd carry my groceries in a basket,
and when my basket was filled, I'd return to our apartment on the
Grand Concourse. The hit man would relieve me of it, take the
basket from my hands as he'd meet me at the door. He would
always be there, waiting, when I returned from grocery shopping.

Together, we'd unpack. Cans and jars in cabinets, perish-
ables in the refrigerator, but he'd do all the cooking. He'd cook
pasta—fedellini, vermicelli, capellini, Acini de Pepe. He'd make
sauces from ripe tomatoes, olive oil, spices. Making sauce would
be an all-day affair.

He'd remain respectful that I don't eat meat, but he wouldn't
respect lentils, soy products, brown rice. These are foods the hit
man wouldn't understand. "What is that?" he'd ask. "You eat
that?" And while I might tell him steaming vegetables retains

the nutrients, he and I are of different generations, different places. He'd continue to sauté his greens in olive oil and garlic. He believes garlic prevents sickness and evil. We would sit at a small table in our dingy kitchen, overlooking an alley, clotheslines crisscrossing, to eat the pasta he cooked.

We would be self-contained. No one would ever visit us. No one knows the Bronx. We wouldn't have children. Or pets. Or a television. He would sit in an armchair and listen to the radio, to opera and to jazz. No longer would I listen to rock-'n'-roll, a part of my other life that would have no place in this one. Maybe I'd learn to like Puccini, Verdi, Lionel Hampton.

The hit man would adore me, treat me as if I were made of porcelain, like his mother's dishes, to be handled with care, to marvel over. He'd say daily prayers of gratitude to whichever saint was in charge of such a blessed life.

As it's his habit to quickly apologize—I'm sorry, babe, he says, even when there's no reason to be sorry—we'd never fight. We'd be very, very happy in our apartment in the Bronx. Until one day, one day something would change. He'd be confused by it. "I don't get it. Explain to me. I'm listening," he'd say.

I wouldn't be able to explain it, but whatever it is would grow, grow hard and sharpen, and eventually snap open like a switchblade.

"What happened?" he'd ask. In Italian, he'd ask me, *"che successo?"*

But I wouldn't understand him. I wouldn't know what he was asking. Italian is not my language.

Haircut

"Ponytails aren't happening anymore," the multimedia artist called to inform me. "I'm going to get mine cut off. What do you think?"

Because I had plans of my own to honor the Kessel sisters' decision and dump him, I couldn't have cared less if he went around with a Hare Krishna topknot. "It's your hair," I said. "Do what you want."

Consequently, I expect to find his ponytail gone, but he opens his door and I see he has the exact hair he had before. His ponytail is intact. "What happened?" I ask. "I thought you were going to get a haircut."

"I was. But my barber is gone. Forced out. His shop's been gentrified. Some flake is selling crystals where my barber used to be." He can't say exactly when this happened, when his barber disappeared, because he hasn't been to him for over a year.

"With customers like you," I say, "it's no wonder the guy couldn't make a go of it." Then I suggest he could go elsewhere for a haircut. There's hardly a shortage of places for that. But he expresses opposition to froufrou salons. "I like a barbershop," he says. "With a striped pole out front, and inside redolent of hair tonic. It's retro."

"There must be other barbershops around."

"But I want my barber." The multimedia artist is close to a tantrum.

This attachment to his barber isn't foreign to me. I have a similar dependency on the woman who cuts my hair. I've also bonded with my gynecologist and my travel agent.

However, circumstances being what they are, the multimedia artist is going to have to buck up, get himself a new barber. Or else live with a passé ponytail.

He puts forward a third option. He wants me to cut his hair. I don't know how to cut hair. I haven't the training, the skill, the natural aptitude, nor the desire to try. "I'd mess it up," I tell him.

"No, you wouldn't. There's nothing to it."

"If there's nothing to it," I ask, "why don't you do it yourself?"

He says he would do it himself except he's unable to reach behind his back and still retain precision.

It seems to me giving a haircut is on the same plane as giving a massage or an enema, also things I'd have to be talked into. We set up shop in his bathroom, carpet the floor with newspaper, put a chair directly beneath the overhead light. He takes off his shirt, and I pat talcum powder on his neck, back, chest. As if I knew what I were doing, I shake out a towel and tie it around him like a bib.

The glare from the light reflects off the scissors. A star twinkles on the stainless steel. The multimedia artist breaks into the rapture by saying, "Let's get on with this, shall we?"

These scissors are not designed for people like me, for lefties. In my right hand, they are awkward. With my other hand, I take his ponytail, lift it up and away from his neck. It's beautiful hair. Thick, black, shines like my own.

The thing to do here is first lop off the ponytail, get rid of it entirely. From there, shape and trim. I position the scissors at the base, above the rubber band. This ought to be as simple as clip, clip, snip, snip. But it's not. I freeze as if some supernatural force were holding me back.

"Is something wrong?" the multimedia artist asks.

"No," I lie. "Nothing's wrong."

"Then cut away." He speaks as if we were doing something harmless.

I cut. I cut again. And again, and his hair, bound in the rubber band, comes away from him. The severed ponytail is as horrible as the pelt of a dead animal. I couldn't possibly break up with him now. I'll have to wait until his hair grows back.

For not acting on the judgment they rendered, I will need to appease the Kessel sisters, like offering the goddesses a gift for ignoring the oracle. I stuff the ponytail into my bag. I will bring it to the Kessel sisters, the way Salome was brought the head of John the Baptist, as if it were proof of something.

Under the Aegean Sky

*A*s if we were partaking in a séance, five couples are arranged—boy, girl, boy, girl—around the table. Weeks ago, my husband and I were invited to this dinner party. Back then, accepting the invitation seemed a lark. It was too far off in the future to contemplate for real.

At my left is a psychologist who avoids looking at me. His wife is a mountain of a woman.

Having hacked at my food enough to give the impression I've eaten some, I push the slices of roast beef to the far side of my plate. Taking another healthy gulp of wine, I eavesdrop on my husband as he discusses renovations on the Sistine Chapel with a woman who introduced herself as a curator at the Brooklyn Museum instead of by name. My husband and this curator babe exchange information from outside sources, what various art historians think of this project.

This—speaking thoughts not your own—is integral to dinner party chitchat. I know this even though I don't have the hang of it. My social skills are lacking. Idle chatter confounds me. Even at the grocery store, when the cashier asks how am I today, I panic. Am I expected to tell her the truth? Do I say miserable? Lost? Confused? Do I ask her the same question?

Across the table, a woman behind a pair of faux marbleized eyeglasses is telling the shrink's wife about the arduous process of choosing a preschool for her intellectually gifted child.

"And how old is little Honore now?"

Honore?

"Five," the mother says. "Five months old."

"Excuse me," I butt in, "how do you know it's intellectually gifted at five months? What does it do?" I am genuinely interested, but neither woman responds except to smile tightly.

I swallow more wine and feel very much like I did when, in my junior year of college, I went to a boyfriend's house for Thanksgiving dinner. This boy had milky skin and no body hair. I didn't want to spend the holiday with him, but he claimed, please, his mother was so eager to meet me.

Picturing him and his mother—just the two of them—eating turkey and canned cranberry sauce at the kitchen table made me so sad, I agreed to go.

Dinner was served not in the kitchen but in the dining room to accommodate him, his mother, me, and the woman and child from next door. The boy's mother surveyed the table and said, "Isn't this nice? A traditional Thanksgiving. Just as our forefathers did it. Turkey with all the trimmings," she gestured at a plate of yams garnished with big marshmallows. "We have family here." She patted her son's head. "And friends." The neighbor and the bratty kid got the nod. "And," she turned a fish eye on me, "a stranger in our midst."

Christian kindness obligated her to give me something to eat just as she would've fed a stray cat.

Because our dinner party hostess aims to be a successful

hostess, and it's bad manners to ignore me for too long, she asks me a question. "Don't you agree it's the fault of television that children no longer read?"

Yes or *No* would do the trick. Either would be a perfectly good answer. But as if I haven't spoken a word in weeks, as if I've been confined in solitary, words accumulate, mount, increase pressure, and burst forth, unleashing a torrent without punctuation. "You can't blame television because there were always alternative forms of entertainment before television you had radio and even during the Roman Empire you had the choice to read Ovid or go watch Christians being fed to lions and that wasn't any different from television besides I prefer reading despite having grown up planted in front of *Howdy Doody, Petticoat Junction, Leave It to Beaver, The Beverly Hillbillies*. I loved those Beverly Hillbillies."

To illustrate my genuine affection for *The Beverly Hillbillies*, I do my impression of Ellie Mae: Paw, if I catch him can I wrastle him?

Not one person at this table owns up to ever having seen *The Beverly Hillbillies*.

"Shall we adjourn to the living room for coffee and brandy?" the hostess says.

Sitting on the couch, it comes upon me like the onset of a headache. A dull throb, a rubber mallet thumping in my chest.

The hurt is distant, inexact, but I want it quelled, so I help myself to a refill of brandy.

The third brandy not only masks the ache, but lets me feel a part of things, like I'm having a jolly time with some really swell people, good friends. I feel as if I belong here.

The shrink's wife is talking about her daughter's riding lessons. "She's enthralled with that horse. All she wants to do is ride."

"Young girls have an affection for horses not generally shared by boys," her husband gives his professional take.

"Yes, I've noticed that." The mother of the intellectually gifted infant asks, "Why is that, do you think?"

And I tell her, and everyone else too, why that is: On a small Greek island, adjacent to Paros, is a mountain, the dome to a labyrinth of caves where, according to legend, priests from the world over would gather for two weeks, ostensibly for prayer, but really to drink wine from goatskin bags, whoop it up, let loose, go wild.

The only way to get to these caves, to make it up the mountain to the mouth, is by donkey. Donkeys are sure enough of foot to navigate the steep, rocky paths. Taking groups of tourists up the mountain on donkey backs is a thriving island business.

Our trek began at dawn. It wasn't a long trip, but it had to be made before the sun was high in the Greek sky, before the mercury soared, became too hot to handle. A dozen of us gathered together at the foot of the mountain waiting for our donkeys and our guide. Among us was the English couple. I didn't know them. That is, we'd never been introduced, but I'd watched them on the beach having a terrific spat. She was bent on taking off her bathing suit top, sunbathing topless. The idea of his wife bare-breasted in public was too, too shocking. Positively scandalous. He wouldn't allow it. "It's not proper," he said.

Well, poop on proper. She yanked off the bra and waved it at him, as if it were a red cape.

He turned his back on her and, dramatically, walked into the sea. I'd half expected him to not return, to have gone and drowned himself.

A donkey is nowhere near as fine a beast as an Arabian stallion, a Tennessee Walking Horse, an old red mare, even. Still, there were enough similarities that I was confident in my mount. I straddled the donkey in one smooth move and started up the mountain while the guide hung back helping the others onto their asses.

157

A donkey's back is bony, humped, each vertebra a knob. Bone pressed hard between my legs. By the time we, my donkey and I, began the ascent in earnest, I was very, very aware of the pressure. I was on the verge of an orgasm. I wasn't sure what to think about that. On one hand—why the hell not? And did I even have the power, the wherewithal, to halt the process once it was underway? On the other hand—I was, in a fashion, about to have sexual relations with a donkey.

The mountain loomed larger and larger before me. The sun beat down on my bare shoulders, and under the Aegean sky, I had sexual relations with a donkey. I shuddered, flushed, and then twisted around to see if the others, that prissy Englishman in particular, had noticed. What I saw was this: They were all riding sidesaddle. No legs but my own were spread-eagled over a donkey's back.

I could've stopped right there, swung my left leg to the right, but instead I had two more orgasms before reaching the summit, before entering the cool of the caves.

"More coffee, anyone?" the hostess sounds like, and looks like, a Chihuahua, shaking and wrecked from nerves. "Can I get anyone another cup of coffee?"

I stand up, a little wobbly, and go to the bathroom. I'd like to throw up, but I'm not sick to my stomach. It's that other sickness, the ache, the sharp hunger pang, having mushroomed, screams for me to fill the hollow. With one husband, a handful of paramours, three friends, I ought to be full. I don't know where there's an opening. So I sit on the edge of the tub and hug myself, hug myself tightly, squeeze real hard as if this feeling were a pocket of air I could force out, the way water is forced out from a drowning man's lungs.

Recorded Messages

*T*here's a message for me, blinking 1, on my answering machine. It's from the multimedia artist. This is his message: As of tomorrow morning, I'm going to be out of town for five days. If you've the opportunity, give me a call tonight. Otherwise, I'll speak with you upon my return.

Why, I ask myself, is he bothering to let me know this? If five days passed without seeing him or hearing from him, would I have even noticed?

I call him back, and although we're together only on the phone, clearly I can see him at his desk — a white drafting table kept neat, pristine. No coffee cup rings stain the Formica, no cigarette burns. No dust. No clutter. To the left of his computer is his appointment book, open. The pages are crammed with dates for gallery openings and parties in his tight handwriting.

"So, where are you going?" I ask, for form. It's expected of me.

"Washington," he says and clarifies, "D.C."

"That's nice." Form again.

"Hardly. Who," he asks rhetorically, "goes to D.C. for pleasure? To do what? Look at monuments? Visit the Smithsonian? Stare at dead art? Art," he pontificates, "must be of the here, the now, up to the minute, a living, breathing organism."

"Can't it live on for a long time?" I ask. "Inspire through the ages?"

"Inspire?" he says in a way I'm to understand art is to do no such thing.

I let the subject go for fear of embarrassing us both.

He's going to D.C., he tells me, to mount an exhibit of his work in a Georgetown gallery. "And it looks like they want me to stay for the opening," he says, as if that were a chore for him.

The work being shown is called *Genocide in Five Days*. Each painting, indistinguishable from the next because they all look like splat, features freeze frames, in the lower right corner, of Wile E. Coyote in pursuit of the Roadrunner. When the multi-media artist showed them to me, he instructed I first scan the panels quickly to see the cartoon in action. This will be set to a light show and a recording of drum solos over explosions, tires screeching, jackhammers ripping up sidewalks. The titles of the paintings are: *Rome Razes Carthage*, *The Spanish Get the Aztecs*, *Raping Bosnia*, *Adios Rain Forest*, *AIDS: American Imperialists Destroy Sex*.

"What about the Nazis?" I asked.

"Please," he said. "That's been done to death. Everyone's sick of it."

During the times we're not together in the flesh, I rarely give the multimedia artist much thought. With him away in Washington, D.C., I can't say I miss him, long for him, count the days until his return. It's nothing, then, but an odd coincidence that I find myself walking in his neighborhood, on his block, past his building. However, this isn't the sort of coincidence that delights me, so I scurry around the corner onto West Broadway, where I get bit with the notion to shop, to buy myself something, a treat to have and to hold. This whim rapidly becomes determination. I take store windows in at a glance, as if speed-reading.

Golden shoes, with gold laces that crisscross and tie around the ankle. These are rococo shoes I'd imagine worn by the Muses, the Graces, the Kessel sisters. I hold the golden slipper out to the salesman, ask if he's got them in 6-1/2 Narrow.

Simultaneously I'm hoping he does and does not have them in stock when he returns with a white box under his arm.

The golden shoes fit as only golden shoes can—perfectly. They feel as if I'm barefoot.

The salesman and I wait for my American Express approval code, and he says, "They're fabulous shoes."

"Oh, yes," I agree enthusiastically and add, "I'll never wear them."

"Of course you'll wear them." He lists occasions appropriate for golden shoes: parties, club hopping, cultural events. "With a black dress and these shoes, you won't even need any jewelry. You could even, for the fun of it, wear them with blue jeans."

"Yes, I could. But I won't. I'll never wear them. It's okay," I assure him. "I want them. I'm buying them. It's just that I know I'm never going to put them on."

"Sign here," he pushes the credit slip at me.

At home, I put my golden shoes, still in the box, still in the shopping bag, like a set of nesting dolls, into the hall closet. I put up water to boil for coffee and check my answering machine.

The first call is from the youngest Kessel sister: I'm soooo bored. Are you home? I'm at work doing absolutely nothing. Call me and we can gab.

The second message is from the multimedia artist: Hello. It's me. I've arrived safely and soundly. Just this minute finished putting up the show. It looks very good, sounds right. It's going to create quite a stir. Anyway, I ... uh ... wanted to say hello. I was ... uh ... I miss you.

I rewind the tape, play it again, fast-forwarding the Kessel sister, making her sound like a chipmunk. And I listen, ear cocked, to the multimedia artist: I was ... uh ... I miss you ... uh ... I miss you ... miss you.

Fetching my shopping bag from the hall closet, I take out the box, put the golden shoes on my feet. Golden shoes are meant for dancing to this tune: ... *Uh ... I miss you.*

From Inside the Bone

The very old man sits in his lawn chair on the second-floor landing. He's dressed up—a navy-blue suit, wide lapels, a natty silk tie—as if he were going somewhere. "Hello," he bows his head as I go by.

I smile, return the greeting, and round the stairs to pat Marvin, the yellow dog, on his way out for a walk. It's as if the hit man's neighbors were my neighbors, except I rarely greet my neighbors. I prefer them to be strangers.

The hit man lets me in. I am assaulted by kisses and by the smells from his kitchen. I pull away from him and ask, "What's that stink?"

"Stink?" he's offended. "I made us something special, a delicacy, for dinner. I had to call the old country for the recipe." By *old country* he means Brooklyn.

He puts opera on the stereo, pours us each a glass of red wine. "*Salute*," he raises his glass. He's leading up to something, the way he's being courtly, the way his shoulders roll before he finds the words he wants. "Look," he says, "just hear me out on this. I'm trying to figure a way for us, you know, for us to have a future. I think maybe I should talk to your husband."

Here *talk* could have other definitions, larger, sharper meanings, pointed with implication. I nearly laugh aloud, as if this were a scene from a movie I am watching, a Martin Scorsese movie. But the laugh gets squelched with this realization: I am not watching a movie.

"No," I say. "No, you will not talk to my husband. Not if you ever want to see me again." Threats he gets, comprehends.

Like a prisoner in his one-room apartment, he paces, turning when he gets to a wall. He is tense. "What am I supposed to do then? Wait for you all the time? I'm fucking pathetic the way I wait for you. I hardly go out for fear you'll decide to pop over, and I'll be elsewhere. I'm like a fucking caged animal here."

"That's your problem." I light a cigarette. My hands tremble slightly. Also, I'm a bit thrilled. Anything could happen.

The kitchen timer goes off, a buzzer signaling the end of a round. "Here," the hit man pulls a chair to the table. "Sit. Relax. We'll have a nice meal. We'll eat and talk like two fucking civilized people, okay?"

He leaves me to do what he has to in the kitchen and to compose himself, get rid of the tension, the discontent. He is capable of that, of putting things unpleasant aside, away, behind, to return to me easygoing, breezy.

His face is tinged pink. He beams shamelessly, as if he'd birthed this food he sets before me.

One thing in the hit man's favor: He goes down on me while I have my period. A lot of men won't do that. But the hit man never hesitates. Like a champ, he dives down, laps, slurps, drips blood on sheets, pillows, the wall, until his bed looks like the aftermath of battle—Bunker Hill, Stony Point—as if slaughter had happened. Yet never does his bed look as violent as what's on this plate.

It's a massacre. Flesh flaking, rotting off a jagged bone, the sort of scene homicide detectives come upon and never forget. I back off, recoil, and ask, "What the hell is that?"

"Osso Buco," he tells me.

"In English." I want to know in English, in a language clear to me. Not in nuances, inflections hidden, draped behind pretty sounds.

"Baked marrowbones," he says.

What ever possessed him to offer me baked marrowbones? I don't eat meat, flesh, flesh of animals that nurse their young, flesh of animals that have eyes to see.

"Forget the meat," he instructs. "The best part's the marrow. Succulent. The marrow's the delicacy. Go on, try some marrow." He touches my upper arm to prod me, but it seems like he's feeling me for plumpness, what a tender morsel I'd make.

Even if I were a meat eater, I'd never eat the marrow, just as I'd never eat intestines, brains, tongue, the heart, or kidneys. Some foods are hellish, infernal, depraved.

"Why won't you try it?" he asks. "I spent all day with this."

"I don't care if it were your life's work." I want him to take it away, out of my sight.

The prongs of his fork pierce a dab. "Come on." The hit man inches the dollop towards my mouth. "A taste," he coaxes. "A *piccolino*."

There is no such thing as eating a little bit of marrow. Once you eat from inside the bone, there's nothing quantitative about it.

"Hey, all I'm asking here is for you to try it," he says.

"And all I'm asking," I counter, "is for you to quit hounding me and take this plate away."

"You're not being very nice. Give me a break here. I made this for you, and now I'm a little vulnerable."

165

I lean back in my seat, flick off the stereo mid-aria. Keeping my voice soft, barely above a whisper, I say, "I am sick to death of things Italian. I am sick of pasta. I am sick of anisette toast. Of espresso. This heritage of yours eats people, swallows them whole." Volume and pitch rise as I ask, "Do you know what I want? I want a fucking grilled cheese sandwich on Wonderbread. I want instant fucking coffee. Sanka. Tea. For dessert I want a Yankee Doodle."

"A Yankee what?"

"Get this horror show out of my sight." Such rage is out of proportion to the situation, but this knowledge doesn't stop me. I pick up the plate of Osso Buco and throw it against the wall. The plate, his mother's plate, breaks into pieces. Meat, blood, marrow, bone splatter.

The hit man stares in disbelief. For a short while, he doesn't speak. Then he says, "You cunt."

"Cunt?" I seize the word. "Cunt." I blow it up, exhibit far greater offense than is genuine. "Cunt." I get my coat. All along I'd been searching for an excuse to leave, to escape the thickness, the oppression, and now he's given me one. "Cunt. Nobody calls me a cunt."

"Now, wait a minute," he moves, stands in front of the door, blocks my exit. "Let's forget this. Forget the Osso Buco. It's no big deal. I can make some pasta."

But the Osso Buco is a big deal. He spent the day stirring bones in a pot, plotting to introduce me to the overpowering sweetness, to tempt me into tasting what I must not experience. This complements his desire to pick, suck, eat from deep within my bones, too. "Get out of my way," I kick at the door. He jumps, and I hurry down the stairs.

Grandmother in
Wolf's Clothing

I lied. I don't want a grilled cheese sandwich on Wonderbread for dinner. Out on the street, I'm cold, hungry, and I want something to heat my insides, to warm me, to stick to my ribs and stay with me awhile.

I go to the corner pay phone and call the multimedia artist on the off chance he's back from D.C. early. He's not. His answering machine tells me he won't be back until Tuesday. I don't leave a message, and with my last quarter, I call the Kessel sisters. "We're not in right now," their machine says, "but if you'll leave your name and ... "

I have no more change to call the love of my life, ask him to have dinner with me, but that's okay because he'd only say no. He doesn't do anything on the spur of the moment. His ways are planned as if he's got a map of his destiny spread out before him.

What I end up doing is this: I head east, crosstown, to Second Avenue, to the B&H Dairy deli, to have noodle pudding or blintzes or potato latkes.

As a result of the cold of the night, the windchill factor, coupled with assimilation, gentrification, a changed neighborhood, the B&H is deserted save for one other customer. An elderly woman at the counter is bundled up like she just got off the boat from Latvia. A wool scarf covers her head, ties under her chin. She wears a heavy brown coat and pile-lined boots on very small feet. She is plump, round, has lipstick on her teeth, and she eyes me in a way that's neither friendly nor suspicious. Rather, for the time being, she defers judgment.

I sit on her right, two stools between us, and smile at her. "Cold out," I say.

"You young girls," she says, "a shortie skirt you wear on a night like this. You'll freeze your *tuchis* off. Where are the brains God gave you?"

I'd rather not get into it, how I hadn't planned on dining alone in a drafty dairy deli, that I was supposed to be snug in my Italian lover's apartment where my short skirt was excessive. Instead I say, "You are so right. I don't know what I was thinking."

"Vell," she acquiesces, "*kayn aynhoreh*, you got the legs for it. Some of them I see with the shortie skirts...." Her hand goes to her cheek, her eyes turn to the heavens. "Like me," she says. "Could you imagine me in such a skirt like a band-aid?"

She's above false flattery. I will not patronize her, will not, in a tone reserved for small and stupid children, say, "Oh, you could wear one." What I do tell her is: You're better off. Believe me. It's cold.

Suddenly, as if something has happened, something I missed, her attention diverts. "So where's the service here? Yoo-hoo," she calls out. "Service would be nice."

From behind the kitchen doors, the counterman shuffles out. "I vant kasha varnishkas," she yells at him. "And tea."

I wonder if he's hard of hearing, and when he pauses in front of me, my voice goes loud, my mouth movements exaggerate. "I'm not sure what I want, but I'll have tea while I decide."

"The kasha varnishkas here aren't half bad," my counter-mate tells me, confidentially speaking.

Our tea comes in glasses none too clean, sugar cubes on the side. I hold the glass with both hands, easing the numbness from my fingers. The woman drinks her tea, sugar cube poised expert-ly between her front teeth.

How lovely it would be to slide over two stools, put my arms around her fat waist, rest my head on her bosom, have her stroke my brow, and say, "Tell me, *bubbeleh*, what troubles you." I want her to take me home with her, to her Second Avenue apartment where she'd cook *tsimmes* for me, stewed fruit—apri-cots, raisins, prunes—on a gas stovetop, and she'd tell me stories about her girlhood in the Ukraine or Lodz. I want her to be the grandmother I never had.

Not that I never had a grandmother. I did have the two of them, but even while they lived, they weren't the sort of grand-mothers this one would be. My real grandmothers would've sooner lived in Calcutta than the Lower East Side. They never lit Shabbos candles, didn't tie scarves around their heads, *schlepp* shopping bags, speak Yiddish.

Grandma Paulette, my father's mother, preferred I not stand on ceremony with her. "Call me Paulette, darling." Paulette was a flashy dame. She favored gold lamé pantsuits, wore her hair—honey blond—in an ornate pile, a crown upon her head. For entertainment, she smoked cigarettes, ballroom danced, played mah-jongg. She took her meals out.

My other grandmother did live on the East Side, the Upper East Side. When I visited, she offered me one of two things to eat: a half of a grapefruit or a vanilla wafer. She shopped at Alt-man's, lunched at Schraft's, played piano sonatas, never raised

169

her voice. She was third-generation American and might as well have been a Quaker.

The counterman steps from the kitchen for no reason other than to have a look, but I take the opportunity to tell him, "I'll have the kasha varnishkas, too." It's a dish I've never eaten before. Or even set eyes on. But I trust my new grandmother, value her opinion.

"Not half bad," she approves.

Her kasha varnishkas arrive, and I sneak a peek to see what it is I'll be having. Noodles shaped like bowties, scalloped edges, mixed with wheatgerm or Maypo. The steam rises, snakes from her plate. A smell wafts my way.

The odor is dissipated by a blast of cold air. She and I both turn to the door. A man and woman, a couple, come in. The man has a fake fur hat on his head. The woman looks a lot like my new grandmother here, except thin.

"Sarah."

"Eppie," the newcomer answers.

Obviously, they're acquainted. Whether or not they have affection, fondness, for one another I can't determine. However, Sarah and the man take the two seats on Eppie's left, leaving no vacancies between them.

"So," Eppie nods in the direction of, but not to, the man, "who's he?"

"My husband," Sarah says.

"Your husband? I thought your husband was dead, may he rest in peace."

"He's not dead. He's right here."

"Nah, I could've sworn your husband passed away years ago." Grandma Eppie is not swayed by evidence to the contrary.

"He's alive." Sarah turns to her husband and asks him, "You

breathing?" The husband doesn't answer, but still, Sarah's satisfied. "He's not dead."

"I could've sworn your husband was dead."

My hand covering my mouth isn't enough to hold back the
giggles. They erupt, squirt through my fingers, and Eppie, Sarah,
and the husband lean forward. Deliberately, they look at me.
Their faces are deadpan. "And who's this?" Sarah asks.

Other than the few words I've picked up on the boardwalk
at Brighton or along Orchard Street, I don't know Yiddish. But
I understand, "*shiksa ... dresske ... pupik ... yentzer.*"

Eppie tells her chum I am not a Jew, I'm just some tramp in
a skirt up to my belly button.

The counterman slides my food at me, as if he considers me
unclean. I hunch over the plate, to be alone, intent on my meal.
Good food to fill me.

Shoveling a forkful of kasha varnishkas into my mouth, I am
not prepared for the sour taste, like something gone bad, food
that's turned on me. I spit what's in my mouth into my napkin,
ball it up, and hide it under the plate.

The Confidence Game

*D*inner, I have figured out, is not in the cards for tonight. But because I told my husband I wouldn't be home until midnight, and it's just after nine, I stop off at a bar. To come home early raises the same questions coming home late raises. Also, a brandy will soothe me and my sore feelings, allow me to forget how hungry I am.

I find I'm seated next to a woman I know vaguely. Kristine, Krista, Krystel. One of those names is hers. She acts pleased to see me, excited even. Her demeanor is that of the mineral water she drinks—bubbly, effervescent, without kick. She is telling me about her trip to San Francisco, how clean it is there, how the people are so friendly.

I am spared from having to respond to this because I catch her eyeing the bartender's butt. Steering the conversation to one of mutual interest, I say, "He's none too shabby in the sack, either."

Her nerve endings go *boing!* The silver ball ricochets madly, bouncing off bumpers. She lights up. "Really?"

"Really," I say.

"So what happened? Why aren't you still with him?"

My affair with the bartender was short-lived because after sex, in those minutes when you're expected to talk, share a thought or a feeling, we, the bartender and I, didn't. "Still," I say, "he's worth a tumble."

She sighs with exaggerated resignation. "I'm involved with someone. We're practically engaged."

"Yeah? Is that so? I was married for seven weeks when I had the bartender. Practically my honeymoon."

She inhales this information as if she were a vacuum cleaner sucking up a mound of dirt. "Are you seeing anyone now," she asks, "besides your husband?"

I hold up two fingers. A *V* like for victory. "Do you know ..." I mention the multimedia artist by name.

"Yes! No! Yes, I mean, I don't know him personally, but I know his work. He's brilliant. What's he like?" She's so perky, her nipples are erect. I assume she means what's he like in bed, so I tell her, "A drip."

"So why do you see him then?" she asks, and I lie, "Because of who he is."

She nods. To have a lover who is famous in certain circles is nifty.

Mistaking this talk for the beginning of something, a rapport between us, she moves in closer, brings her bar stool within an inch of mine, as if we're in cahoots. There were men who responded to me similarly, assumed a bond because I'd slept with them one lousy time, as if sex were something unique, special, not commonplace. "This guy I'm involved with," she confides, "he's really nice to me. And he makes a good living. He'll be a great husband, but you know what I mean...." She does not want to come out with it: He's a sexual dud.

"So have more on the side."

"That's not as easy as you make it sound," she says, and I beg to differ. "Yes, it is." I swallow my last drop of brandy, and Kristine, Krista, Krystel reaches for her wallet. "Let me get a round here."

"No, thank you. I have to go." I do not want her to buy me a drink.

"Hey," a great idea springs to her mind—snap—like a rubber band. "Let's get together on Saturday. Go shopping. Have brunch."

"I'm busy," I say without regret. Nor do I offer an alternate date, not even *some other time.*

Undaunted, because she's certain these confidentialities carry weight, depth, she takes a cocktail napkin from the stack. "What's your phone number?" Her pen is poised, ready to write. "I'll call you."

This is a rule of mine: Do not give out your phone number willy-nilly.

Heart Failure

*T*he multimedia artist is dead. He died. He died from heart failure. I read this in the newspaper, the *Times*, which was delivered, like an omen, to my door. It is my multimedia artist who is dead. Not some other multimedia artist. I am sure of this because his picture is printed along with his obituary. This is jarring because judging from this photograph, we could be twins, and I am looking at the death of me.

His obituary reads like an abridged version of his résumé, enumerating shows, exhibits, performances of his work. "The art world has suffered a great loss," is a direct quote by the attending physician who pronounced him dead from a ruptured aortic aneurysm, the result of a genetic abnormality in the structure of the vessel. The multimedia artist is, was, must have been, more famous than I realized.

Because I'm not sure exactly how an aortic aneurysm ruptures, I imagine his heart blew like a bicycle tire punctured by a shard of glass or a sharp stone. And here I'd been cursing him through and through for not calling me upon his return. I'd been worried, distressed, he might dump me before I had the chance to dump him, that his message claiming to miss me was a cruel setup. Now I know he didn't call me because he died at the age of thirty-seven on the D.C.-to-New York shuttle.

The way an EKG or a polygraph test makes tracks, lines, chicken scratches, thoughts etch across my mind, the sort of thoughts I'd think if he weren't really dead: Heart failure? I didn't know he had a heart. Figures it was a defective one. He'd die knowing a failure of his was written up in the *Times*, even if it is only his heart and not something the critics have a go at. On the other hand, he'd be very, very pleased, smug, to learn he was given such a lengthy and prominent obituary, the sort of thing he'd clip out, xerox, and include in his publicity kit.

I wonder if he had the foresight to draw up a will, and did he bequeath me a little something? Maybe he left me those atrocious panels of red dialogue. After all, I did inspire them. They might have sentimental value for me. And if they don't, they're bound to be worth a nice piece of change. The art world is that way. There's nothing like the artist's untimely demise to quadruple the value of the work.

The obituary concludes with this note: Funeral services were held at the Minneapolis Center for Reform Judaism.

The funeral is over, done with. His body is in the ground. Jews, even Reform Jews—a group nearer in thought to a social organization than a religion—don't wait for the body to cool before burying it.

Had I learned of this death earlier I might've gone, not to that Reform Center, but to the cemetery. I picture a lone Jewish cemetery in Minneapolis as old, disheveled, stones crooked and craggy, like cemeteries in decaying mountain towns. A few old Jews would be huddled around the grave, braced against the cold Minnesota winter, which is like the winters in Warsaw, the winters of their youth, their home.

A year from yesterday there will be the unveiling of the headstone. I note the date, fix it in my memory. There are three hundred and sixty-four days remaining to gather together the pieces before they'll scatter once again. I have one year, shy of a day, to figure out if I am grief-stricken over his death, or am I only feigning grief? Time and distance allow for the ripple effect to happen and quell. In a year from now, I should know where this disturbance has come to rest upon me, my life. It ought to become clear to me if we, the multimedia artist and I, were truly beginning to care for one another, if we were reaching out toward an understanding, perhaps love. Or did, indeed, our hearts fail us?

In Black and White

Overnight, it snowed. It is the first—and so late in the year possibly the last—snowfall of the season. From the kitchen window, I look out over the hushed courtyard. The trees appear metallic, the ground crisp, white against a gray backdrop. This could be Vermont, Maine, Bialystok, a place serene, a place where I don't belong.

I move from this window to another window, the living room window. Here, there is a different view altogether. The snow is muddied, ground to slush, tromped through, walked over, yellowed from dog pee. Only the sky is the same. A deep slate sky, as if this snow were not over with, as if, at any moment, it will begin to snow again. Such a sky renders all below it a photograph, a still photograph in black and white.

It is the kind of day that urges me to telephone the love of my life, to invite him to bed, to say, "I'll bring strawberries, champagne." He would, I'm certain, refuse the strawberries, the champagne, the sex. As if I were a darling child, but nonetheless a headache of one, he'd say, "Now, now. You know that isn't to be."

It isn't to be because he has forbidden himself pleasure. He lives, survives, on desolation and sorrow. It is his devout belief that he has no right to a good time.

Still, I never give up on him entirely. I might periodically back off, but retreat is not the same thing as surrender. So I might press on and ask, "How about a cup of coffee, then? Could I entice you, on this gloomy day, to meet me for a cup of coffee?"

"You entice me every day," he'd spout some debonair and goofy throwaway line. I love that he bothers with such things even in the face of reality. The reality is: I do not entice him every day. I rarely entice him, and especially not when the sky is blue and the sun is yellow. Other than those times at the movies, when we met inside the theater where it was dark, we meet exclusively on rainy days, or late on a November afternoon when everything is shaded in periwinkle. I have never seen his face bathed in sunlight nor felt a warm touch from his hands.

The love of my life lives in a black-and-white world. He dresses in grays, or beige. Noncolors, banishing so little as a green stripe in a tie. And of course, he is dead set against the colorization of movies. He has written articles by the ream denouncing the process, the results. It's as if he doesn't want there to be color to anything. Not even the flowers or birds or butterflies. The only color he allows for is the sporadic slash of red, having expressed fondness for my lipstick.

Once, in an attempt to highlight for him what an erotic picture we would make, I told him, "Together, we look as if we stepped out of some film from the 1930s, where although you never see it, you know the man and woman portrayed are kinky, depraved. We look like that, as if we get off on you strapping my wrists and ankles to bedposts."

179

"Do we?" He asked as if he didn't know.

I pick up the telephone, hold the receiver to my breast, and dial his number when a shaft of sunlight cracks the slate sky. Before he answers I hang up, because suddenly the day is no longer laid out in black and white.

Early the Next Morning

*A*s if the sunshine of the day before warmed the world, a hint of spring murmurs through the morning air. Fresh, dewy with promise. On telephone wires small birds hop and cheep sentimentally.

I'm not able to appreciate any of this. Groggy, cranky, I haven't had my morning coffee yet because I am out of cigarettes. One without the other is unthinkable.

I turn left and instinct, something primal, warns me: Beware. Danger, trouble, lurks in the next doorway.

"I need to talk to you," the hit man jumps out at me.

I've never seen the hit man in the morning, the early morning, until now. It's anachronistic. A black storm cloud against the expanse of blue sky. He hasn't shaved. He sports the stubble of a five-o'clock shadow, and it occurs to me he's been there, in that doorway, for days and nights, waiting for me to come out. I do not ask him if this is so because I don't want to be saddled with the lengths he goes to.

"I'm a cunt," I remind him. "Why do you want to talk to a

181

cunt?" On the surface I keep cool, but I'm rattled. Parts of me shake. My ribs chatter like false teeth. My heart pounds. I don't like the way he's crossed into my territory, planted himself on my turf when no one was looking, the way Chinatown has encroached onto Mulberry Street.

"Where are you going?" He lopes alongside me.

"For cigarettes," I tell him, but I walk past the kiosk.

"I can't take it without you," he says. "These days without you are killing me. Apart from you, I'll die."

As that has happened more than once—away from me for a while and then men turn up dead—I don't dismiss this claim outright, but nor can I listen to it. I clamp my hands over my ears.

"Come on," he pulls one of my hands away. "Listen. Please. Please, let's talk. Don't walk away from me. I need you. Listen, what have I got left here? Twenty-five, thirty years on the outside?" He speaks of his own mortality as if he were a bookie, as if I should wager a C-note against his life. "Thirty years without seeing you, I wouldn't make it. Without seeing your face, hearing your voice, lapping your hoochie."

Lapping my hoochie. That kind of talk melts me. I bite my lip.

"Look at me," he asks. "Please look at me."

Even if I wanted to look at him, I wouldn't. I'm not myself yet. I haven't put on my makeup. I'm not prepared to face the world or the hit man.

"You know," he says with the precision of a prophet, "you're as beautiful without makeup as you are with it. A different kind of beauty, but still you steal my breath away."

"For a cunt." I won't let it drop. I can't let it drop. It's all I've got to keep some distance between us.

"Cut me some slack here, would you? I'm sorry. I'm really sorry. I was upset."

I ignore him, and not knowing what to do or where to go, I

head for the subway. He follows me down the steps to the IRT, but he doesn't have a token with him. I drop mine into the turnstile and lose myself in the crowd on the platform.

"Listen," he's at my side again the way a nagging conscience won't let you alone either. "You're the only woman I've ever loved. I'm not going to let you get away."

"Let go of me," I demand, although he isn't touching my person.

"No," he says, "I won't let go of you. Not ever."

A train pulls in, and in the push and shove of passengers getting off and on the train, I manage to separate myself from the hit man. He calls out to me over the rush-hour commotion, "Don't go. Please, don't go. Stay with me."

I'm safely on board, and the train coughs, jerks, lurches, but instead of pulling out, the doors open again long enough for the hit man to squeeze in next to me. He takes my hand in his as the train leaves the station destined for Flatbush Avenue, Brooklyn.

Forfeit the Kiss

On my way out, I stop to check my mail. Bills I leave for my husband. The picture postcard is addressed to me. It's a glossy photograph of a snow-covered mountain congested with towropes and ski lifts. A red banner—*Ski Utah*—cuts a man off at the knees. It's from the Kessel sisters. They have gone to Utah to hit the slopes. *Utah*? This card is an absurdity, makes no sense. The Kessel sisters don't ski. The youngest one has been known to whimper in the cold, to beg for warmth. And why didn't they tell me they were taking a vacation? Or invite me to join them?

Halfway down the block, I tear the picture postcard into thirds and litter the pavement with the pieces.

I walk as if guided by a force not my own. My steps are heavy with resignation. The truth is: I'd prefer to turn back, go home, be alone. I don't want to be with the hit man, but I haven't got the spunk to tell him so. Right now, as much as I dread it, to go to him is easier than to break our date or end our affair. Too bad I didn't hang tough, stick by my words: *Nobody calls me a cunt.* Instead, I let him worm his way back into my life.

184

I allow him to kiss me before brushing by him to fall, plop, into the armchair. "I must be getting old," I say. "I barely made it up those stairs. I'm pooped." Then I tell him, "The Kessel sisters have gone to Utah, to go skiing. They didn't invite me to join them."

"So what?" the hit man says, "You wouldn't have gone, would you? Would you?"

"I guess not. Still, doesn't it strike you as odd? The Kessel sisters skiing in Utah?"

"Ah, fuck them," the hit man doesn't want anyone else, not even talk of anyone else, to intrude on us.

I yawn. "I am really tired," I yawn again.

"I'll make you coffee." He is eager to serve me. "A strong cup of coffee. You want?"

"Yes," I say. A jolt of caffeine might pick me up, restore energy for whatever action is ahead.

As if I'd lapsed from consciousness, I find him standing before me, holding out a cup of coffee. I haven't the steam needed to extend a hand to take it from him, nor the strength to hold it, lift it to my lips. "Put it down," I mutter. My eyes shut, struggle open, and shut again, as if I were being hypnotized, as if the hit man were swinging a pocket watch in the rhythm of a metronome, intoning *You are getting sleepy. Very sleepy.* "I don't know what's wrong with me," I say. "I'm exhausted."

"My poor baby," the hit man oozes sympathy. "You had a hard morning?"

"No." There's no explanation for this fatigue, but the desire to sleep overwhelms me, narcoleptic in intensity. "I ought to go home." I push at the armrests, to hoist myself up and out, but I don't make it. I slip back into the armchair as if it were a poppy field.

"Here," the hit man turns down his bed, pulls back the spread, fluffs the pillows. "Come on," he says. "Sleep. Have a nap."

We both know perfectly well what transpires when I'm in his bed, that we do things unrelated to napping. "I promise," he holds up his hands to prove they are empty, that there's nothing up his sleeve. "I won't touch you. Go ahead. Sleep."

Sleep is too tempting to resist, and I let him help me out of the chair and into the bed. He pulls the covers over me, smoothes them out, tucks me in. "Sweet dreams," he kisses the top of my head.

My eyes close and sleep washes over me like the tide over sand. I drift into it, thinking: Sleep. Sleep. I want to sleep and sleep for hours.

It is possible I am dreaming, except I'm sure I am not. I feel the hit man's touch on my cheek. I hear him whisper into my ear. "Sleeping beauty. My sleeping beauty," and I bolt upright. I'm wide awake, alert, and alarmed. How foolish I was to trust him. I dare not, must not, ever go to sleep in the hit man's bed. I would sleep too deeply, and that son of a bitch would forfeit the kiss, the kiss designed to rouse me from my slumber, just so he could keep me here, holed up, with him always.

Everything Passes

*F*irst there was the fatigue. Now there's a tickle in my throat. An itch I can't scratch. My muscles ache. I grow warmer, then shiver. My eyes are glazed as if I were medicated.

When things get set into motion, when mass is multiplied by velocity, they gain momentum. And then, according to Newton's Law of Gravity, whether it's an apple falling from a tree or a man from a window, only an immovable force—such as the ground below—can stop it. Or, as in my case, a bed. Once a flu begins its course, all you can do is prepare for it to hit.

I arrange things: I throw an extra blanket on the bed, locate the remote control to the television, get undressed and into the paisley print flannel pajamas purchased months ago with this, succumbing to a flu, in mind.

The hit man answers his phone before the first ring is completed, as if he were hovering over it the way a vulture circles a dying cow.

"I'm sick," I announce. "I've got the flu."

"Oh no. Oh, damn. Babe, I'm sorry. I am so sorry."

187

"It's only a flu," I impress upon him. "I'm not about to perish."

"Yes, yes. Of course. You'll recover. You'll be fine. *Passe tutti*," he tells me. "Everything passes. So," he says, "I guess this means you're not coming over today."

My teeth grit together. "That's right. I won't be coming over today."

"Do you need anything?" The hit man asks if he can bring me aid, comfort, supplies. "Aspirin? You got aspirin. Soup? Hot soup is good. Juice? You got juice in the refrigerator?" Sometimes the hit man forgets I have a husband, that I do not live alone.

"Yes, I have plenty of juice. I don't need anything." I thank him for offering though, and I promise to call him if I find myself wanting.

He hems and haws, pauses before asking, "What about tomorrow? You think you'll be well enough to see me tomorrow? What about it?"

"Everything passes," I tell him.

I write my husband a note: I've got the flu. Don't wake me. Please pick up a couple of quarts of orange juice and a bottle of aspirin. Thanks. Love.

I leave the note on the kitchen table and look in the cabinets to see if I do have a can of soup. The hit man was right. Hot soup would be good, but there isn't any. If the Kessel sisters weren't skiing in Utah I would ask them to make me some soup, the three of them to stir the cauldron.

Time, days pass like this: I sleep. A restful sleep, deep, as if I were an innocent. Intermittently I wake to pop aspirin, drink juice, catch snippets of *General Hospital, Jeopardy, The Love Connection*. It's a cat's life.

On this third day, instead of getting better, my flu takes a turn for the worse. My fever shoots up, soars high, higher, as if my blood were bubbling. My mouth is dry, my lips crack. I suppress a cough for fear of spitting up blood. I worry that this is not a simple flu I've contracted but scarlet fever, tuberculosis, double pneumonia. Seemingly healthy people can die with little, or no, warning. From out of the dark a stray bullet can hit.

I slip, not into sleep, but from a conscious state to delirium. I dream of things that are not dreams. Things too real to be dreams, too vivid, and besides, I'm not sleeping as I watch three white bunny rabbits scamper up a mountain where, on the peak, haloed in a glow, the old woman from the B&H, that grandmother in wolf's clothing, juggles Ukrainian Easter eggs as if they were hot potatoes. "*A zoy geht us,*" she says to me.

"Speak English," I tell her. "Speak to me in English."

"That's how it is," she translates. "See how it is," and there is a mirror in my hand, my left hand, an old-fashioned mirror with a silver handle.

I expect to see my reflection, but it is the multimedia artist who gazes back at me. "Bad timing," he says. "I'm booked solid this week, but let me check my calendar. Maybe I can squeeze you in." He disappears from the mirror, and the love of my life is here, at my side, in my sickbed. He kisses my forehead, my eyes, my mouth, my neck. Kisses like lemon drops. I take his hand, bring his fingertips, his palm, his lifeline to my lips. Along the interior of his forearm I kiss, one by one, each of the six numbers tattooed vertically on his basilic vein. These numbers are all that survived from his childhood.

Everything goes black, and I can't find him. I call for him to come back to me, and a bright light flashes, like an explosion but without sound. I can make out the World Trade Center in the distance, and I watch as I tumble out a window but do not land.

I weep for what's been uprooted, for what is gone, for what I can't bring back. And when I wake my face is wet from tears and the perspiration of a fever breaking. My head is clear. The ache has vanished. I am well again. Not just better, but healed, saved.

The hit man is grateful to learn I've recovered, pulled through intact. "I've missed you," he says. "I've missed you something awful. For days I've been walking around with this enormous hard-on. When can I see you? I need to see you." He is desperate for me to say *Now, this minute, I'll be right over*, but I explain that wouldn't be prudent. "I'm probably still contagious."

"Fuck prudent. I want to catch your germs. Even your germs are beautiful to me, and I want them. I want all of you."

"Yes," I say. "I know that. And while it's noble of you, it's also stupid. This flu is a whopper. Trust me," I tell him. "You don't want it."

"I see," he says, and I wonder if he does see, does he know it's over, it's all over, that he won't have me again, ever.

Stepping into the shower, I let the spray rinse away sweat, sleep, nightmares, visions. The water runs over me for a long while until I am refreshed, cleansed, baptized. I towel dry, get dressed, and go out.

Across the street from his building—the no-frills, Communist Bloc-type highrise the love of my life calls home—is a schoolyard. There, I lean against the chain-link fence. My arms are spread like wings, but rather than aiming to take flight, I hold on and watch a cloud drift across the sky. Sparrows dart from one telephone wire to another as if landing were only a springboard for taking off. Traffic flows, cars change lanes. People walk to and from their destinations. But I, an anomaly against the flux, the immobile force, remain still, embraced in the sunshine until, like everything else, daylight passes.